Jeremy Strong once worked in a bakery, putting the jam into three thousand doughnuts every night. Now he puts the jam in stories instead, which he finds much more exciting. At the age of three, he fell out of a first-floor bedroom window and landed on his head. His mother says that this damaged him for the rest of his life and refuses to take any responsibility. He loves writing stories because he says it is 'the only time you alone have complete control and can make anything happen'. His ambition is to make you laugh (or at least snuffle). Jeremy Strong lives in Kent with his wife, Susan, a cat or two, and something in the attic that makes scratching noises at night, but he hasn't found out what it is yet.

Jeremy Strong

The Shocking Adventures of Lightning Lucy

PUFFIN BOOKS

PUFFIN BOOKS

Published by the Penguin Group
Penguin Books Ltd, 80 Strand, London WC2R 0RL, England
Penguin Putnam Inc., 375 Hudson Street, New York, New York 10014, USA
Penguin Books Australia Ltd, 250 Camberwell Road, Camberwell,
Victoria 3124, Australia
Penguin Books Canada Ltd, 10 Alcorn Avenue, Toronto, Ontario, Canada M4V 3B2
Penguin Books India (P) Ltd, 11 Community Centre, Panchsheel Park,
New Delhi – 110 017, India
Penguin Books (NZ) Ltd, Cnr Rosedale and Airborne Roads, Albany, Auckland,
New Zealand
Penguin Books (South Africa) (Pty) Ltd, 24 Sturdee Avenue, Rosebank 2196,
South Africa
Penguin Books Ltd, Registered Offices: 80 Strand, London WC2R ORL, England

www.penguin.com

Lightning Lucy first published by A & C Black 1982
Published in Puffin Books 1993
Text copyright © Jeremy Strong, 1982
Lightning Lucy Strikes Again first published by A & C Black 1985
Text copyright © Jeremy Strong, 1985
Lightning Lucy Storms Ahead first published by A & C Black 1987
Text copyright © Jeremy Strong, 1987

This collection published as *The Shocking Adventures of Lightning Lucy* in Puffin 2002
6

Text copyright © Jeremy Strong, 1982, 1985, 1987, 2002
Illustrations copyright © Rowan Clifford, 2002
Illustrations based on the original artwork of Nick Sharratt © Nick Sharratt, 2002
All rights reserved

The moral right of the author and illustrator has been asserted

Set in Baskerville MT

Made and printed in England by Clays Ltd, St Ives plc

British Library Cataloguing in Publication Data
A CIP catalogue record for this book is available from the British Library

ISBN 0–141–31419–2

Contents

Lightning Lucy

1 Can Four Year Olds Fly?

Nobody thought there was anything special about Lucy until she fell into the garden pond. Lucy was just four at the time. Before that happened, Lucy's mum, Mrs King, had thought that Lucy was just a nuisance and messy and noisy – but not extra-special. Mr King thought Lucy was sweet, pretty and a little imp – but not extra-special. Lucy's two-year-old brother, Nicholas, didn't think about his sister at all and neither did the family cat, Flop.

But that was before Lucy fell into the pond. It wasn't a very large pond, but it was right in the middle of the garden. It had a rockery and clumps of stunted flowers around it. Mrs King kept trying to grow pretty little rock-plants, but

Lucy spent so much time mountaineering on the rockery that it didn't look like anything much at all. The pond wasn't very deep, but it was deeper than Lucy was tall. There were real fish in it, and frogs, and great floating, weedy leaves that had snails underneath them.

This particular day was warm and sunny. There wasn't a cloud in sight and Lucy had spent most of the morning running around the garden doing helpful things, like pulling up the flowers and shoving them in the pond because she thought they needed water.

A small plane flew overhead and began to twist and dive and zoom up in the air and roll over. Lucy was fascinated. She stood in the sunshine and watched the plane go through all its aerobatics. It was just as if the pilot was putting on a display especially for Lucy. The plane came tumbling out of the sky, rolling over and over directly above her. She took a couple of steps back to keep the plane in view, and with the second step there was a tremendous splash and she disappeared into the pond.

Water streamed over the sides and dribbled down the rockery. All that could be seen of Lucy was a pair of dirty white socks and muddy sandals sticking out of the water, kicking furiously. Mr and Mrs King, who had been sunbathing, dashed towards the pond to haul their drowning daughter out.

Suddenly a fountain of water exploded upwards, soaking them both. Lucy rocketed out of the pond, her arms stretched out above her head, trailing long streamers of green weed. She zoomed straight up into the topmost branches of the apple tree, clasped her arms round a branch and began to howl dismally.

Mr King stared up at his daughter, frozen with shock. Mrs King pinched herself hard, to make sure that she hadn't been seeing things. Lucy wailed from the top of the apple tree. Her father swallowed and gulped.

'I'll get a ladder,' he said, and hurried over to the garden shed. He put the ladder against the tree, climbed up and carefully carried Lucy down. She was still crying. Mrs King took her inside to dry her off.

It was twenty minutes before Mr King had a chance to talk to his wife, because she was busy putting Lucy to bed.

'She was shocked, Harold,' said Mrs King.

'I'm not surprised. I was too. Didn't you see what I saw?'

'I don't know.' Mrs King wrung her hands. 'I don't know what I saw.'

'Surely you saw what I saw!' cried Mr King. 'Didn't you? Tell me what you saw first.'

Mrs King bit her lip and stared anxiously at her husband. 'I just don't know, Harold. It all happened so quickly.'

'That's just it,' exclaimed Mr King. 'If it had happened slowly, it would all make sense. You don't want to tell me what you saw because you can't believe it, can you? Well, I'll tell you what I saw. There was a whoosh of water and our Lucy came flying out of that pond. Don't screw your eyes up like that, Elsie, she was flying. Flying, and there were weeds trailing from her arms and legs.' Mr King had jumped up and was marching nervously round the room.

'She'd gone sort of red,' added Mrs King in a quiet murmur, as if she still could not believe it. 'There was a sort of red glow all around her.'

'Lucy wasn't red,' said Mr King. 'It was a glow all around her.' Mrs King nodded.

'And then,' continued Mr King in a matter-of-fact kind of voice, 'she flew up into the old apple tree and sat in the top branches and cried.'

'The glow went first,' said Mrs King. 'The glow faded as she landed in the tree.'

'There,' said Mr King. 'You saw exactly what I saw.' There was a long silence as the two worried parents stared at each other. Mrs King began to cry.

'I don't understand it,' she sobbed. 'Children can't fly, Harold. At least they shouldn't. I mean, who taught her to fly? They don't teach flying at school nowadays, do they?'

Mr King sat down next to his wife and put a comforting arm round her. 'Perhaps we just dreamed it. Maybe it never happened at all. It could simply be that . . .'

'But we both saw it!' wailed Mrs King. 'Our Lucy, flying through the air!'

Mr King sighed. 'I'll telephone for the doctor.'

Mrs King gave a tearful smile and asked, 'Is he coming to see us, or Lucy?' Mr King laughed and patted his wife's shoulder.

'I don't think we're that mad. He ought to see Lucy. She could catch an awful cold from that ducking.'

By the time the doctor called, it was mid-afternoon. Mrs King had put young Nicholas in his cot for an afternoon sleep, but Lucy was wide awake and running about as if nothing had happened at all. Dad wouldn't let her play in the garden and that made Lucy angry.

'Why can't I?' she kept asking, tossing back her curls.

'Because you may fall in the pond again.'

'But I've never fallen in the pond!' protested Lucy. Mr King stared at her.

'Surely you remember falling in the pond?'

Lucy shook her head crossly. At that moment the doorbell rang and Mrs King let the doctor in. Dr Evans was quite young. He was a good doctor with children and Lucy liked him.

'Hallo, young Lucy,' he said. 'Have you got the measles again?' Lucy smiled and shook her head. The doctor turned to look at Mr and Mrs King.

'We're a bit worried about her,' began Mr King. 'I think you'd better go out and play, Lucy, while we talk to the doctor.'

'Outside?' repeated Lucy.

'Yes, but keep away from the pond.' They

watched Lucy run out into the garden. Dr Evans smiled as he watched her go.

'She seems to be in the best of health. I can't think what's worrying you about her.' He sat down in an armchair.

Mr King sat down on the sofa next to his wife. He grasped his hands firmly in his lap and looked straight at Dr Evans.

'Can four year olds fly?' he asked. Dr Evans blinked several times and raised his eyebrows with much surprise.

'I beg your pardon?' he said at last.

'We want to know if four year olds can fly,' repeated Mrs King, and she went on to tell the doctor the whole extraordinary story of Lucy and the pond.

Dr Evans listened without saying a word. He just sat back in the armchair with his mouth dropping further and further open and his eyes getting rounder and rounder. His hands gripped the arms of his chair and when Mrs King had finished he said quietly, 'Could I have a cup of tea, Mrs King?' He gave a funny sort of laugh and scratched his head rapidly. The poor doctor seemed very confused.

'It's an odd story,' he said at last. 'I'm sure

there must be a good explanation for it.' He tried to smile.

'Yes?' asked Mr King, waiting for the good explanation.

'I'm trying to think of one,' said Dr Evans desperately, and he gave that funny, nervous laugh again. Mrs King broke the long silence that followed when she brought in the tea. The doctor sipped at his cup gratefully.

'Let's have a look at Lucy, then,' he suggested. 'She must have something to show for all this.'

Little Lucy could not understand why Dr Evans wanted to examine her. 'I'm not ill,' she kept saying. 'There's nothing wrong with me.'

'Are you still ticklish?' asked the doctor. Lucy put her head on one side.

'Only sometimes,' she replied, grinning.

'What's all this I hear about you falling in the pond this morning?'

Lucy stamped her foot impatiently. 'I didn't,' she said angrily.

'Oh well, maybe you didn't,' agreed Dr Evans amicably. 'You know something, Lucy? I think you're the healthiest person I've looked at today. I can't find a thing wrong – not a spot or a bump or a lump! But,' he added, narrowing his eyes so that Lucy looked at him anxiously, 'I bet you're still ticklish!' He gave Lucy a quick tickle and told her to go back outside and play. Then he turned to Mr and Mrs King.

'There's not a mark on her. She's a perfectly normal four year old. I can't find anything wrong at all.' Mr King started to say something but Dr Evans interrupted. 'I know this is difficult for you but it seems to me that you both saw something extraordinary happen to Lucy. She says nothing happened. I think that something peculiar did happen, but it happened to both of *you*, not to Lucy. You had a sort of shared dream, a very real dream: so real that both of you are sure it actually happened.' Dr Evans looked from one to the other. 'It's the only sensible explanation I can think of,' he added, as he packed his little case.

Mr King stood up slowly. 'Thank you for coming, Doctor, I hope we haven't wasted your time.' Dr Evans frowned and smiled at the same time.

'Not at all. It's been most interesting.' He shook hands and left. Mr King went back to his wife, shaking his head.

'It wasn't a dream,' insisted Mrs King. 'It really happened.'

For a few days after that, the Kings kept a special eye on Lucy but nothing happened to her. As the weeks passed both parents began to wonder if they really had dreamed the whole thing. Lucy became five, six, then seven and still nothing happened.

Now the Kings had almost forgotten about her flying, simply because they didn't want to remember it. But then something happened that started the whole thing all over again.

2 Something Extra-special

Lucy King was now almost eight. Many things had happened since she fell in the pond. She was taller and looked even wilder than before. Her long, red curls rampaged down the sides of her smudgy face. Lucy always appeared to be dirty and Mrs King despaired of keeping her clean. She was forever mending and washing and taking a damp facecloth to Lucy's hands and face. Then she'd rub hard while Lucy squirmed and struggled.

'I just don't know how you manage to get yourself so dirty,' sighed Mrs King, a few days before Lucy's eighth birthday.

'I'm not really dirty,' said Lucy, rubbing at the streaks of dirt on her suntanned arms. 'I could get a lot dirtier, only I do try to keep clean.'

'I don't believe it!' mocked her mum.

'I do. I can't help it if there's dirt on the things I touch.' Lucy sniffed. 'People should keep them clean.'

Mrs King scrubbed hard at Lucy's cheeks. 'I don't see how you can keep mud and puddles and bits of old iron and useless car tyres clean,' she said. 'Those are the things that you play with and they'll always be dirty. Why don't you play with your friends and do clean things? I never got dirty when I was a child. We had too many good games to play.'

'I've got good games,' protested Lucy, trying to get away from the facecloth.

'I don't think rolling in the mud is a good game unless you happen to be a hippopotamus, Lucy. And I don't think making camps inside dustbins is a good game either. Now listen, it's time you did your piano practice.'

'Oh no!' wailed Lucy, and she pulled a hideous face. At that moment Nicholas poked his small, dark head round the kitchen door. He grinned up at his sister.

'Piano practice,' he reminded her. 'Don't forget your piano practice.'

'You wait, Nicholas,' shouted Lucy, still struggling beneath the facecloth.

Lucy had been taking piano lessons for two months. At first she thought it would be great because she would be able to play brilliantly straight away. In actual fact it was a lot harder than that. She was still finding it difficult to read music, let alone play it with two hands. Mum and Dad made her practise for half an hour every day and she hated it.

'I'm going to play in the garden,' announced Nicholas loudly, just to make Lucy jealous.

'Don't tease your sister,' said Mrs King. 'It's really not fair, Nicholas.'

Lucy stuck out her tongue and pulled another revolting face. Nicholas stared at her thoughtfully.

'You know that competition on TV about drawing a wild animal and you can win a bicycle?' he began.

'Yes? What about it?' muttered Lucy, with her face still twisted up horribly.

'Well, if you pull that face again, I'm going to draw you. Then I'll send it in. It's bound to win. I think I'll call it Wild Girl of the Woods. When they see it, they'll probably send an animal catcher round to get you and take you to the zoo or something.'

'Ha ha, very funny,' sneered Lucy. 'Why don't you go and fall under a lorry?'

'Lucy!' cried Mum, quite horrified. 'Don't ever say things like that! That is a terrible thing to say to anybody, especially your own brother.'

Lucy was taken aback. She hadn't thought it was *that* awful. She and Nick were always saying things like that to each other. In fact they had a game they sometimes played where they tried to think of the most awful things that could happen to each other. Lucy reddened.

'Nick knows I didn't mean it,' she mumbled. Mrs King sighed.

'Don't call him Nick. His name is Nicholas.'

'But that takes ages to say,' complained Lucy. 'I mean, if there was a fire or something and you had to tell Nick, I mean Nicholas, something quickly, by the time you'd called out his name he would have got all frazzled up!' Lucy grinned at the thought.

'Don't be stupid,' snapped Mrs King. 'I don't know, first you want him run over by a lorry and now he's being burned to death. For goodness' sake go and get on with your piano practice before you think of some other awful ending for poor Nicholas.'

Lucy gave a long groan and stomped off to the front room. She shut the door, sat herself on the piano stool and fiddled with her music. First she looked at one piece and then another, but she didn't play anything. After five minutes of silence from the piano Mrs King shouted through the door. 'Get on with it!'

Lucy thumped out a simple tune with one finger. She had a brilliant idea. If she played her tunes twice as fast, then she should finish twice as quickly. It seemed to make sense, so Lucy raced through six different pieces. When she looked at the clock she was astonished to see how little time had passed. She sighed and stared out of the open window.

Nicholas was outside playing with their cat, Flop. Lucy sat on her stool, her hands idle, watching the cat stalking a twig that Nicholas was trailing behind him. Then he found a conker from the previous year and began to toss it on the grass. Flop chased after it and batted it with her front paws. Lucy forgot all about her piano practice.

Nicholas picked up the conker and threw it

even further. It bounced down the garden path and Flop shot after it. She flicked a paw at the little ball and sent it scuddering under the garden gate and into the road, where it spun round before lurching to a halt. Nicholas opened the gate and ran out to collect the conker, laughing at Flop who was still searching under the gate.

Lucy's little brother did not see or even hear the lorry coming down the road. He was too busy thinking about his game with Flop. There was a shriek of screaming tyres as the lorry driver rammed his foot hard on the brakes, but there was nothing he could do. The uncontrollable vehicle skidded sideways – but it still went straight for the terror-struck Nicholas. An old lady walking on the pavement screeched and covered her face with both hands.

Suddenly Lucy appeared, her flying body shining with a bright red, crackling glow. She hurtled out of the window, toppling the piano stool. With both arms stretched out in front, and her long curls streaming behind, she zoomed down and swept Nicholas from beneath the whirling black tyres of the thundering lorry and carried him back safely to the garden. There she sat on the wall, grinning, while the red glow slowly faded and Nicholas stared up at her, still in a state of open-mouthed shock.

The little old lady took her hands from her face and fainted. The lorry came to a squealing halt and the driver jumped down and ran back to Lucy. He looked at her as if he had seen a ghost. His mouth worked up and down like a large fish's, but for a few moments he could say nothing. At last a stammering cry fell from his pale lips.

'Yu . . . yu . . . you all right?' The driver put a finger on Nicholas and then he touched Lucy to see if she was real. Lucy laughed.

'Yes,' she said. 'Of course we're all right.' She brushed one hand through her curls and there was a faint crackle of static electricity.

Mrs King came hurrying out of the house. Before she had time to ask what all the noise had been about, the lorry driver had told her. Together they picked up the old lady and brought her into the house for a strong cup of tea. The lorry driver had one too, because his legs felt a bit wobbly. Even Mrs King was a bit flustered.

'Like a bolt of lightning, she were,' murmured

the old lady. 'Glowing she were, an' all. Glowing red all over, and sizzling and crackling like I don't know what.'

Mrs King looked out of the window to where Lucy was already playing quite normally with Nicholas. She hurriedly got rid of the old lady and the lorry driver. They kept asking awkward questions and Mrs King did not have any answers. When they had gone she called her children indoors.

'Lucy, tell me what happened out on the road.' Lucy burst into floods of tears.

'I didn't mean it, Mum, really I didn't. I didn't know it would happen!'

'What on earth are you talking about?' asked Mum soothingly.

'She means the lorry,' explained Nicholas.

'But what about the lorry?'

'I didn't know there really would be a lorry trying to run Nicky over,' wailed Lucy. 'I know I said he ought to fall in front of a lorry but I didn't mean it to happen.'

Mrs King smiled and gave Lucy a big hug. 'Don't be silly,' she said softly. 'That lorry didn't come because of what you said to Nicholas. That was just chance. But what actually happened?'

Nicholas began to jump up and down
impatiently because Lucy was still sniffing.

'I ran into the road, only I didn't see this
monster lorry coming. It was going to squash me
but Lucy flew out of the front room and picked
me up.'

'I'm sure you don't mean that Lucy *flew*, do
you, Nicholas?'

'Of course I do!' he cried. 'She flew and she
was all flashing red. It was very exciting, Mum, I
wish she'd do it again.'

Mrs King had become silent so Lucy went off
quietly because she didn't want anything to
remind Mum that she hadn't finished her piano
practice. Dad got the whole story from Nicholas
and Mrs King as soon as he got in from work.
He asked Lucy about it too, and this time she
remembered everything. Lucy wondered why
everybody was making such a fuss about it all. It
seemed quite natural to her. If somebody was
about to get crushed by a lorry, you rushed out
and saved them.

'But, Lucy, dear,' said Mrs King, 'children
don't fly and glow red.' Lucy shrugged her
shoulders.

'I can't help that. I mean, there's a boy at

school called Richard and he can make both his ears waggle. He makes them go up and down and they wriggle and nobody else in the whole school can do that. I mean, you could say that children can't waggle their ears, but Richard can. He does it every playtime.' Lucy looked up at her parents and smiled. 'Anyway,' she added, 'it didn't make me dirty.' Mr King laughed but Mrs King shook her head.

'I think I would prefer it if you did just get dirty. At least I can understand that.' She sighed heavily. 'Oh well, let's have tea.'

That evening when both children were in bed, Mr and Mrs King talked for a long time.

'There's no explanation for it, but it's happened again,' said Mr King. 'It's not a dream. Our Lucy has something special, something extra-special.' Mrs King nodded slowly.

'I suppose we shall have to put up with it,' she said. 'But I do wish she could just be ordinary for one minute.'

3 Nicholas Takes Off

Mr King folded his newspaper, took off his reading glasses and looked across at Mrs King. 'I've just thought,' he said, 'do you remember when Lucy was six months old?' Without looking up from her work, Mrs King nodded. 'We were on holiday,' continued Mr King. 'We went out one afternoon for a wander round that little fishing village. Do you remember how it got terribly dark because of that sudden storm?'

'The thunder!' said Mrs King. 'And the lightning too. It was right above us, wasn't it, and it all started when we were in that little shop that sold those shell-thingummies. What were they?'

'Flower-pot holders.' Mr King leaned forward

and tapped his wife on one knee. 'Now tell me,' he said with a secretive smile, 'where was Lucy?'

'Where was Lucy?' repeated Mrs King. 'In her pram of course.'

'But where was the pram?' demanded her husband.

'It was outside. I remember it well because when the thunder and lightning started we rushed out to her and just as we got to the door . . .' Mrs King trailed off into silence and for a few moments she stared at her husband. Then she whispered, 'Do you think that was it?'

'It could be,' said Mr King. 'There's got to be an explanation somewhere for Lucy's strange power.' His wife leaned forward eagerly.

'There was that awful clap of thunder right overhead wasn't there, Harold? I thought it was the end of the world. Then an enormous flash of lightning and the whole of Lucy's pram seemed to glow and there was that dreadful sizzling noise. We rushed out to the pram and when we looked in, she was lying there and laughing. Do you remember?'

'I do, I do,' said Mr King. 'And then it simply poured. We were soaked and had to rush for the car. We even came home a day early.'

The couple looked at each other. 'It must have been that,' said Mrs King at last. 'There has to be a reason. Do you think Lucy's getting worse? All sorts of odd things have happened since she rescued Nicholas. She doesn't seem different herself, but things have happened.'

'What sort of things?'

'Nothing much, just little things. I keep going into rooms and getting a strange prickly sensation in the back of my neck, especially in Lucy's bedroom. It feels as if somebody is tweaking my hair from behind, but there's never anybody there. Yesterday I came out into the hall from the kitchen and I'm sure I saw a flash of red hurtle up the stairs, just like a ball of fire.'

'Ball of fire?' exclaimed Mr King. 'Perhaps it was Flop chasing something.'

Mrs King eyed her husband patiently. 'Flop is hardly like a ball of fire, dear. She's an old, fluffy black and white cat. That's not what I saw at all.' Mr King grunted. It was too puzzling.

'Hmmm. Well, I don't suppose it had anything to do with Lucy. It's her work at school that worries me. Her teacher says she's a lazy chatterbox who hardly ever reads and does the most awful, scruffy work.' He broke off and groaned.

'Well, I don't find that at all surprising,' said Mrs King. 'She's exactly the same at home – untidy and lazy.'

They both began to laugh and Mr King said, 'It's obvious that she hasn't changed at all!'

Lucy King had changed though. Ever since she had rescued Nicholas she had felt different somehow. At first she didn't think that there was anything special about flying and having crackling hair, but so many people seemed to think it was odd that Lucy found herself wondering about it more and more.

Early one morning she found herself alone at the adventure playground. She stood beside the swings and dreamily wondered if she could zoom over to the climbing frame, which was some distance away. Hardly had she thought it than she was there, standing next to the climbing frame as though nothing had happened. She wasn't even out of breath. Lucy watched the flickering red flush fade away. To test herself further, she ran as fast as she could back to the swings. She arrived, several seconds later, panting as furiously as a tortoise at the

Olympic Games. When at last she got her
breath back, she flew in an instant back to the
climbing frame and once more watched her
fiery radiance slowly disappear. For the first
time Lucy realized what she could do, and she
was delighted.

Over the next week or so, Lucy did her
zooming act in private whenever she could,
though once Mum nearly caught her flying up
the stairs. What Lucy did not know was that her
wonderful powers made her capable of doing
other things besides flying. She soon found out
though.

One day she was upstairs in her bedroom,
struggling to make a camp out of bedclothes by
stretching them over an open cupboard door.
Nicholas kept wandering in and out. He was
being a bit of a nuisance.

'I can make a better camp than that!' he kept
saying.

'Good. Go and make one in your own room
then,' snapped Lucy.

'Can't I come in yours?'

'No.'

'I'll let you use my bow,' said Nicholas.

'I don't want your bow, I'm not Robin Hood.

I'm me, and this is my camp and I want to be alone.'

'You won't be able to catch any food without my bow and arrow,' insisted Nicholas slyly.

'Look,' cried Lucy angrily, 'if I get your bow I'll shoot you and eat you. Go and play with a crocodile or something.'

'I want to come in your camp,' whined Nicholas, and he came nearer.

Almost without thinking, Lucy raised her arms and pointed her grubby, nail-bitten fingers at her brother. She did it in desperation, trying to keep him out of her private camp. Her hair stuck out at all angles and her body gently throbbed with a vivid red glow. Her eyes shone like black stars and tiny flickers of lightning sparked from her fingertips.

Nicholas found himself lifted from the ground and floating round Lucy's bedroom. She wasn't touching him, just pointing at him and grinning. Nicholas hovered over the chest of drawers. He kicked his legs and wailed.

'Put me down! Mum! Mum! Tell Lucy to put me down, it's not fair!'

There was a pounding of feet on the stairs as Mrs King hurried up. She ran into Lucy's bedroom and threw up her hands at the sight of Nicholas hovering round the room. She gawped at her son and then stared at Lucy who sat, quietly glowing, just inside her camp.

'Lucy!' cried her mum. 'Is this your doing? I might have known. Let Nicholas get down, please.'

Lucy gave her mum a bright smile and then concentrated her strangely glowing eyes upon Nicholas. She made him do a double slow-motion somersault in mid-air and then landed him safely on the wardrobe.

'Not up there!' shouted Mrs King. 'On the floor, at once!' Lucy brought Nicholas down to ground level, where he immediately began to wail. The red glow vanished and Lucy shook out her curls with a tiny shower of sparks.

'I only wanted to go in her camp,' sobbed Nicholas, clutching at his mum.

'It's really too naughty, Lucy,' said Mrs King sternly. 'You mustn't play cruel tricks like that just because you have special powers. It's very unkind. You can stay up here until I call you for tea.' Mrs King pulled Nicholas out and shut the door with a bang.

Lucy retreated deep into her cupboard-camp

and looked closely at her hands. She was
delighted. Anyway, why should Nicholas and
Mum be so cross about it? She couldn't help it.
She hadn't meant to make Nicholas float like
that. It had just happened.

Lucy idly pointed one finger at her teddy. He
took off slowly and then zoomed upwards. He
cruised round the room and finally dived out of
one corner and landed in Lucy's lap. She hugged
it closely. A voice shouted up the stairs, 'Lucy!
Tea-time!'

She went down and sat at the big kitchen
table.

'Say you're sorry to Nicholas,' said Mrs King.

'Sorry, Nicky,' said Lucy, helping herself to
some bread.

'Not Nicky! How many times do I have to tell
you? His name is Nicholas.'

'Muhmuhmuss,' mumbled Lucy through a
mouthful of bread and jam.

Mrs King once more turned on her daughter.
'Your manners are dreadful,' she scolded. Lucy
eyed her, wishing that she dared to make her
mother float across the table and round the
room like her teddy had just done upstairs. Mrs
King almost laughed.

'I know what you're thinking, Lucy King, so don't you dare. If you can do special things you make sure you keep them for the right time.'

Lucy frowned. 'I can't even think in this house without someone knowing all about it.'

'Never mind. Have some more bread,' suggested Mum. 'You're being very quiet, Nicholas.'

'I've got tummy-ache,' he said, looking at Lucy with a meaningful stare.

'I'll give you some medicine,' said Mum, reaching up into the cupboard. The small brown bottle was wedged behind the best teapot. As Mrs King pulled it out, the pot got pushed to the edge of the shelf and toppled over.

'No!' cried Mrs King in horror.

Lucy calmly raised one sparking finger towards the falling pot and the fat teapot stopped, a few centimetres above the stone tiles. Lucy made the pot turn up the right way and then she flew it three times round the room before allowing it to land gracefully on the kitchen table.

Mrs King let out the long breath she had been holding all this time.

'Thank you, Lucy,' she said at last.

'It was a special occasion,' said Lucy.

'Yes, it certainly was. I don't think you had to make it fly round the room so many times though. That was showing off.' Lucy blushed and looked down at her jam sandwich. Nicholas began pointing at the teapot, jabbing at it with each of his fingers in turn.

'Why can't I do it?' he demanded.

'I think one person in the family is quite enough for that sort of activity,' murmured Mrs King. 'Absolutely enough.'

4 The Christmas Angel

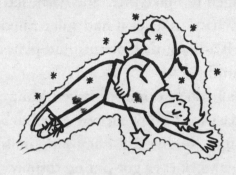

Lucy enjoyed school except for two things. One was work and the other was Maureen Best. Lucy didn't know why Mr Barber, her teacher, made her sit next to Maureen. Maureen was one of those girls who seemed to be brilliant at everything and it made her rather big-headed. The two girls didn't like each other at all. Maureen thought Lucy was the biggest clot on earth and Lucy said Maureen looked like a mouldy apricot.

The whole school was preparing for Christmas. Decorations were being put up everywhere and each class was making something. Lucy got quite involved.

'Look,' said Maureen one dark afternoon.

'I've made six of those bell-things.'

Lucy looked at the bells jealously. She had only managed to make one. She had tried desperately hard and yet it had still turned out looking as if a herd of elephants had played football with it.

'Is that all you've done?' smirked Maureen. 'It's all squashed. I don't suppose Mr Barber will hang that up.' Neither did Lucy suppose so. None of her work ever got put on display.

Maureen held two of her beautiful bells up to the light and swung them from side to side. 'Really, Lucy, you can't do anything. I suppose you want me to give you one of my spare bells? Well, if you give me all your crisps at playtime tomorrow you can have this one.' Maureen held up a rather crumpled bell. Even crumpled, it looked a lot better than Lucy's, but was it worth a whole packet of crisps?

Lucy saw Mr Barber coming round, choosing the bells to decorate the classroom. She glanced back at Maureen's bell.

'All right,' she said, and hurriedly put the bell in front of her. Maureen grinned and sniffed at the same time.

'Don't forget tomorrow, the whole packet!'

Lucy nodded and gritted her teeth. It was blackmail. Why did she have to sit next to the mouldy apricot?

Mr Barber came and stood behind Lucy. He bent down and looked at her bell.

'Well done,' he said, sounding surprised. 'You must have tried very hard, Lucy. It's lovely to see you making such an effort.' Each one of his words grated on Lucy's nerves and she wished she had never made the exchange at all. Maureen sniggered to herself while Mr Barber took the bell away and hung it up.

Lucy shut her eyes and wished that she could make Maureen Best float up into the sky and disappear for ever. She hoped Maureen would choke on the crisps.

Mr Barber began talking to the class about a Christmas play he wanted them to perform. He needed several actors. The announcement got everyone excited.

'Sssh,' said Mr Barber calmly. 'It's not easy to act. Some of you will have speeches to learn.' Lucy waved both hands wildly in the air. She just loved acting and having lots of people watching what she was doing, and she knew she could be brilliant at it.

Mr Barber wrote down the names of all the children who wanted to act and then he set about testing them. He gave them a piece of writing to read out loudly from the back of the class. 'Pretend you are on stage,' he suggested. 'I want to hear a nice loud, clear voice.'

One by one, the children read. Some did it well and some were even better. Maureen was one of the best, of course. Some children were quieter than rioting snails. Then it was Lucy's turn. She spoke up really loudly because she was desperate to get herself a speaking part. Mr Barber clapped his hands over both ears.

'There's no need to shout that loudly,' he interrupted. 'They'll hear you in China!' The class thought this was hilarious and Lucy turned deep red. After that she could hardly speak at all. It came out in a nervous whisper. Lucy knew she wouldn't be chosen and felt totally miserable.

Mr Barber didn't tell the children which ones had been chosen until the next day. Maureen got the part of the Angel Gabriel and the rest of the speaking parts went to other children. Lucy's was the last name to be called. She'd been given the part of a dumb angel. Lucy groaned. That meant she'd have cardboard wings and a halo made from a tin-foil pie-dish. She'd have to look saintly the whole evening. That wasn't acting at all. Maureen brushed past.

'I'm the Angel Gabriel,' she beamed. 'Have you got those crisps?' Lucy handed over the packet without a word. Maureen examined it carefully.

'They're all broken!' she complained. Lucy looked up at her.

'Oh,' she sighed, 'but you're so clever, Maureen. Surely you can stick them back together again?' Maureen's eyes narrowed, but she could not think of an answer and turned on her heels and clicked away.

Every day now there were rehearsals. Mr Barber got crosser and crosser as children could not remember their lines or did the wrong thing. Mothers at home busily made costumes. Mrs King made a superb angel dress for Lucy and her dad made a splendid pair of golden wings out of gold foil paper and thick card. It was a lot better than Lucy had imagined and she got quite excited by the idea of her costume and the performance. Then there came a bitter blow.

Mr Barber announced that the Angel Gabriel was going to use the brand-new flying wire that the school had recently bought for the stage. There was a gasp of envy from the rest of the class and Maureen grinned like a drunken pig. The flying wire was a belt with a wire attached that went to a strong beam in the ceiling. If you buckled the belt round your waist, you could be hoisted safely up into the air over the stage, so that it seemed you were really flying.

Of course, everyone had wanted to try it, but Maureen was going to be the lucky one.

'Why does everything happen to her?' whispered one of the naughtiest boys.

'Because she's such an angel, of course,' answered Lucy quickly, and she flapped her hands like a pair of wings. The boy laughed, but they were both still envious, even when Maureen found it difficult to speak because the belt cut into her lungs. Her face went rather red.

'She's not the Angel Gabriel,' Lucy told her mum. 'She's the Beetroot Gabriel.'

The day of the performance came at last. The excited children watched the school hall fill with parents – a real, live audience. They dashed back to their classes to get their costumes on. Mr Barber checked the flying wire to make certain it was safe. The audience went quiet as the hall lights were dimmed. The curtains were pulled aside and the play began.

Everything went well to start with. Only once did a shepherd forget a line. There was a short pause and then one of the other actors covered up for him. Mr Barber breathed a sigh of relief. It was almost time for the angels to go on. He tightened the belt round Maureen's waist.

'Good luck!' he whispered and started up the machinery to hoist Maureen over the stage.

Then it all went wrong. The machinery jammed solid and would not budge. The actors on stage waited in tense silence for the Angel Gabriel to lead the other angels on. It was supposed to be the highlight of the show, with the Angel Gabriel flying high above the cast. The audience waited, knowing that something had gone wrong. Mr Barber threw up his hands in despair.

'It's no good,' he said. 'You'll have to go on just as you are.' At this point the Angel Gabriel burst into loud sobs because she felt so let down.

'Pull yourself together!' hissed Mr Barber anxiously, while the whole cast waited. 'These things happen. Just go on as you are.' But Maureen cried even louder.

Lucy had a horrible thought. If she wished, she could make Maureen float up to the ceiling after all. Then everybody would see the wailing Angel Gabriel with tears smudging her very un-angelic face. No, that would be nasty. Lucy tugged at Mr Barber's sleeve as he sent the other angels on stage to keep things going.

'I know all Maureen's lines,' she murmured. Mr Barber gazed at her for a second. He made his decision and smiled.

'Good girl, Lucy. Are you sure?' Lucy nodded. Mr Barber patted her halo.

'Right, on you go then!' Lucy grinned up at her teacher. It was an enormous grin, from one ear to the other.

'Not on,' she said. 'Up!' Mr Barber's eyes bulged like stupefied marbles as Lucy rose gracefully into the air and flew slowly across the stage with her hair sparkling just like a real halo.

Then she began her speech, hovering over everyone's head. She did it marvellously. When she finished, the audience actually cheered. They thought the flying was very effective and didn't realize the machine had broken down. Mr Barber was the only one who knew the truth. Lucy flew across the stage several times while the audience clapped continuously. At last she flew off, closely followed by the cast.

As soon as she got backstage Lucy asked, 'Where's Mr Barber?' She wanted to find out if her performance had been all right.

'Oh!' cried one of the other angels. 'He fainted when you took off. He's been taken to the staffroom to lie down.'

Mr and Mrs King, who had been in the audience, had also hurried to the staffroom to see Mr Barber. When they had seen Lucy fly across the stage they knew instantly that there was no machine holding their extraordinary daughter up, especially when she did it three times.

'She's a show-off,' whispered Mrs King to her husband.

'So would you be if you could fly,' replied Mr King with a proud smile.

In the staffroom they had an urgent, hushed conference.

'We want it kept a secret,' explained Mrs King. 'We don't want Lucy to get big ideas about herself.'

'We'd rather as few people know about her powers as possible,' said Mr King.

'Of course,' said the white-faced teacher. 'I'm not sure I believe what I saw myself.'

Back in the hall the play ended triumphantly. The audience clapped and clapped. Maureen had already been taken home with an awful headache and had missed the fun. Back in the classrooms the children changed out of their costumes and talked excitedly about the performance.

'What was the flying machine like, Lucy?' asked one of her friends.

Lucy was just going to tell them all that had really happened when she saw her parents coming through the door. She frowned for a moment.

'Well, the belt was a bit tight,' she said quickly. 'But I managed.'

'You were brilliant,' one of them said. Lucy blushed deep red.

Mr King laughed and shook his head. 'I don't know, Lucy. Whoever would have thought you'd be a success as an angel of all things!'

5 The Outing

Lucy came home from school very excited one day. She burst through the front door and ran to the kitchen, where Mum was peeling potatoes.

'Mum! Mum! We're going on an outing and we need sandwiches and a drink – only we can't take tins and it costs £3 and Paula says I can sit next to her so we can share sweets – only I mustn't take barley-sugars because Paula doesn't like barley-sugars and . . .' She drew in a deep breath.

Mrs King put down the potato peeler and waited for quiet. 'I don't know how you manage to think about what you're saying, Lucy. It comes out like a volcanic eruption. Calm down and tell me again. Where are you going?'

'To the Priory Museum.'

Mum nodded. 'And when are you going?'

'Next Monday, and I've got to wear my best clothes,' said Lucy.

'I should think so too. What are you going to do at the museum?' Lucy looked blankly at her mother. 'Don't you know? Surely Mr Barber told you?'

Lucy thought for a moment. 'I think so,' she said at last. 'I think he said something about stinking eggs and hairy manners but it didn't make sense and that's why I didn't listen.' Mum began to scratch at the potatoes again.

'Really, Lucy, you are useless. You don't listen to a word. It goes in one ear . . .'

'And out the other,' interrupted Lucy. 'I know, Mum. You keep telling me.'

'I'd better give Paula's mum a ring. Perhaps Paula listens to Mr Barber when he tells you things.'

'That's because she's a goody-goody and always gets everything right,' said Lucy quickly.

Mrs King went to the telephone and spoke to Paula's mum for several minutes. Lucy heard her laughing. When Mrs King came back to the kitchen she was still smiling. She gave Lucy a playful clump on the head.

'You really are the end, Lucy. Honestly, what did you think you were going to see at the museum – "stinking eggs and hairy manners"? Mr Barber said that you are going to see extinct hairy mammoths and a lot of other fossils too.'

'Oh!' said Lucy, idly making Mum's potatoes fly slowly over the table and land with little plops in the pan of boiling water on the stove. Mrs King gave a long sigh.

'I do wish you wouldn't do that. I find it so muddling, Lucy. I'm just not used to flying potatoes yet.'

'Sorry.' Lucy dragged herself out of the kitchen.

It seemed ages before Monday came. Lucy had packed everything she needed at least two days too early. Mum refused to make the sandwiches until the night before. Lucy insisted on helping, so it took twice as long.

On the Monday morning the class crowded on to a big coach and spent five minutes sorting out which seats they wanted. All the boys wanted to go in the long seat at the back, but Lucy didn't mind where she was. Mr Barber and two parents came in the coach too. It was exciting, and Lucy kept bouncing up and down in her seat until Mr Barber told her to sit still before she bounced out of the window.

Lucy thought it was better being in a coach than in a car because she could see over all the hedges and walls.

'That's the bakery,' Paula pointed out. 'My uncle works there.'

'What does he do?'

'He puts the jam in doughnuts.'

Lucy looked very surprised. 'He doesn't do it very well,' she said. 'He must get jam all over his trousers and the floor too because he keeps missing.'

Paula was puzzled. 'What are you talking about?' she demanded.

'Well,' said Lucy with a big grin, 'when my mum buys doughnuts there's just a hole in the middle. There's no jam in them at all!'

'You're mad!' cried Paula. 'Those are ring-doughnuts, not jam-doughnuts. Ring-doughnuts have holes and jam-doughnuts have jam . . .' By the time Paula had finished explaining they had reached the museum, and the tour began.

There were all sorts of odd things to see.

There were fossil elephant teeth and bones and old flints that had been used as axes and spears. There were lots of drawings, too, that showed how people had lived thousands of years ago. Lucy peered closely at a painting of a hunting expedition.

'I bet Nicholas would have liked to be a stone-age hunter,' she said. 'He could have used his bow and arrow then.'

'They didn't have bows and arrows,' said Paula briskly, busily writing lots of notes in her pad. 'Look at that sabre-tooth tiger,' she added. Lucy gazed at the model of the extinct creature, with its enormous front fangs poking down the sides of its lower jaw. Mr Barber gathered the class around the animal.

'Why do you think it had teeth that long?' he asked them all.

'I bet he didn't like going to the dentist,' whispered Lucy to Paula, but her friend didn't even laugh.

'They didn't have dentists in those days,' she answered seriously.

'I know that!' cried Lucy. Really she wasn't *that* stupid.

'Did you say you know, Lucy?' asked Mr

Barber in surprise. 'Can you tell us why the sabre-tooth tiger had such long teeth?' Lucy blushed and stared wildly all over the museum. She suddenly remembered a TV programme about how parrots used their beaks for climbing through thick, leafy trees.

'Did they use them for climbing trees, Mr Barber?' she suggested brightly.

There was loud laughter. Even Mr Barber smiled.

'I don't think so,' he said. 'They were used for killing their prey.'

So the tour continued. Lucy began to think she would die of starvation if they didn't stop for lunch soon. At last they were allowed to go off to the little cafeteria and eat their sandwiches. 'I helped make these,' said Lucy with pride as she opened her sandwich box. Paula glanced inside.

'I can see that,' she agreed. 'They look bigger than bricks.'

After lunch there was little time for further exploration. Lucy was quite pleased because her legs ached. She was glad to get back on the coach. The journey back took about an hour, and it was up and down all the way. There was one exciting bit that Lucy enjoyed, even when she was in her dad's car. There was a particularly steep hill.

On the way to the museum you had to go up and round and up and round and the coach would get slower and slower until you thought it would start going backwards, but eventually it always got to the top. On the way back to school it was like diving off a mountainside because the coach would go steaming down the hill at breakneck speed and the driver would keep stamping on the brakes to slow the heavy vehicle down.

That's what the coach driver was doing today. He kept pushing at the brake pedal. He kept pushing and pushing and his face turned green and then white. Mr Barber leaned forward, gripping the shuddering hand rail in front of him.

'What's the matter?' he asked.

'Brakes gone!' croaked the driver, plunging his foot up and down on the useless pedal. 'We haven't got any brakes!'

'Can't you do something?'

'I'm trying! I'm trying!' shouted the driver. Sweat poured from his face. 'Nothing!' he cried. 'We're getting faster and faster. We can't take the next bend at this speed. We're going to crash!'

Mr Barber leaped into the swinging aisle of the coach.

'Listen,' he yelled above the rising whine of the tortured tyres. 'Do what I say immediately. Lie down on the floor and wrap your arms round your heads. The coach is out of control. Get down on the floor immediately.'

The children started screaming at each other, but they did as Mr Barber had told them, all except for Lucy. She stared out of the front window in horror, watching the sharp bend racing relentlessly towards them. Paula reached up and tugged at her.

'Get down, Lucy!' shouted Paula.

'Oh shut up!' said Lucy, losing all patience. She desperately tried to concentrate on the coach, trying to make it stop. Somehow she could not make it work. Nothing she did had any effect upon the hurtling tonnes of metal. She struggled from her seat, clutching at the seats around her, for the coach was lurching violently from one side of the road to the other.

'Get down!' yelled Mr Barber from beneath his seat, but Lucy ignored him. She hauled herself to the front, right next to the driver.

'Let me out,' she said. The driver didn't dare

look up as he tried to keep his grip on the shaking steering wheel. 'Let me out!' shouted Lucy. The driver gave a wild laugh. He thought Lucy was trying to escape.

'Won't do you any good jumping, miss,' he shouted back. The corner was getting closer and closer. 'This is it!' the driver yelled.

Lucy's frantic eyes suddenly noticed the button marked DOOR amongst the driver's controls. She lunged forward and banged it with her fist. The door hissed open and the wind came screaming in. Before the driver could open his mouth, Lucy had zoomed out of the coach.

She rocketed forward, hovering a few metres in front of the coach. Her hair stuck out straight, with masses of sparks scattering through the air, and she glowed as she had never done before. Power surged through her small body and passed out through her spread hands. She concentrated her whole being upon slowing down the helpless vehicle. The whole coach seemed to become enveloped by the flickering radiance that surrounded her body.

Gradually the coach slowed. The driver's eyes were riveted upon the vision of the glowing girl floating in front of him. He felt the control of the vehicle coming back. Mr Barber and the children struggled from the floor and sat in their seats. They could not take their eyes off Lucy hovering in front, still guiding the coach. Even the crying had stopped. At last the coach halted.

Lucy flew back to the roadside and the red flush faded. She shook her crackling hair back into shape with a shower of dying sparks and climbed up the steps into the coach.

'Lucy King . . .' began Mr Barber. He coughed. Words had caught in his throat. He didn't know what to say. Lucy smiled sheepishly at everybody.

'Where are my brick sandwiches?' she asked. 'I'm hungry.'

6 PRUNO!

Of course, after the adventure with the coach, the secret of Lucy's strange and wonderful powers could not be kept hidden any longer. Within twenty-four hours Mr and Mrs King found themselves answering never-ending knocks at the door and telephone calls. Everybody in the King household got a headache, including Lucy. Mrs King began to wish that her daughter had never been left out in that thunderstorm eight years earlier.

The story of the uncontrollable coach and Lucy's glowing display of flying filled the newspapers for several days. The King family could not move from the house without being questioned by reporters, or photographed. They stayed indoors as much as possible and began to feel like prisoners in their own house.

Lucy wondered how she could have caused so much fuss and the more dismayed her parents became, the more Lucy felt she was to blame. Then, suddenly, one morning all the press men and TV crews had gone. There wasn't a reporter in sight. It turned out that a polar bear at London Zoo had just given birth to a black bear cub and they had all gone to write about that.

However, when the post arrived their peace was broken once more. Letters simply poured through the letter box. Lucy started to get all sorts of requests. A building firm asked if she could use her super-strength to knock down some old houses that needed demolishing. It would save them a lot of time and money. Another letter came from a part of the country that had received no rain for two months. Would Lucy please push some clouds over their bit of the country and hold them there until they had emptied?

There were many more letters asking for help and also several from companies that wanted Lucy to appear on television and advertise their products. Mr King tore them all up without bothering to read them. It didn't stop the endless flood of mail though. The postman didn't bother to push them through the letter box any longer. He just left a sack full of letters on the Kings' doorstep.

One evening they sat at the tea table in gloomy silence. Mrs King sighed.

'I wish we could get away somewhere, just for a little while.' She glanced apprehensively at her husband.

'We can't,' he said. 'We simply haven't got the money.'

'I've got 72p in my money box,' offered Nicholas.

'And I've got 40p,' said Lucy. Mr King gave them a tired smile.

'I'm afraid it's not enough. No, we just don't have the money to go away, especially after that last bill I had to pay on the car.'

Silence spread round the table once more. Mrs King stared out of the window.

'Lucy could get us some money,' Nicholas suggested.

'How?' asked Lucy.

'You could break into a bank with your super-strength and take the money.'

'Ha ha. Anyway, I'm not super-strong. I can only sort of levitate things.'

'Well, levitate the money out of the bank then,' said Nicholas.

'I wish I could levitate a brain into your head,' said Lucy sharply. 'I don't know if you know this, Nicholas, but it's against the law to rob banks.'

'Well, why don't you do one of those adverts on TV then?' persisted Nicholas.

'What adverts?'

'The ones that Dad keeps tearing up. You can get money for that.'

Mrs King sat up straight and stared at her son. 'How do you know all this, Nicholas?' she asked.

'I've read all the bits in the litter bin.'

'Ugh!' cried Lucy, but she was interrupted by Mum.

'Tell us what they said,' demanded Mrs King, eagerly leaning forward. Nicholas thought carefully for a second.

'Um . . . the only one I can remember was about some wallpaper and they said they'd pay Lucy £1,500 for making a TV advert.' Mrs King's eyes widened. She stared at her husband but he shook his head.

'Lucy's not going to make adverts,' he said. 'They'll spoil her and make her feel special. They'll make fools of all of us.'

'But £1,500!' whispered Mrs King.

'I don't mind making an advert!' Lucy cried, jumping up and down.

'We could go away for two weeks!' murmured Mrs King dreamily. 'We could go abroad. Right away to another country . . .'

'In an aeroplane!' shouted Nicholas. 'We could fly!' Lucy groaned.

'I can do that already,' she complained in such a fed-up voice that everybody laughed. Mr King looked from one happy face to the next.

'All right, I give in. Let's have a look at those torn-up letters.'

Mum got some tape and they began to stick the letter-litter back together. An hour later they found what they were looking for. They had read several rather silly offers but this one seemed fairly sensible. A big cereal firm were about to launch a new breakfast cereal called PRUNO. The firm offered Lucy £2,000 to make a TV advert for them.

'£2,000!' cried Nicholas, dancing round the room.

'£2,000!' cried Mrs King as she joined him. Then Lucy began a dance too, while Mr King watched them with a worried smile. He wasn't convinced they were doing the right thing. All the same, he wrote to Nutt & Co, the cereal firm, that same evening.

A week later Lucy found herself on a train, going to London with Mum. They were due at the TV studios to film the advert. They were met at the London station by Mr Nutt himself and he took them off in his silver Rolls-Royce. Mr Nutt was a very friendly fat man. Lucy couldn't help wondering if he was so portly because he had to test lots of cereals. Mr Nutt chatted to the Kings all the way there.

'PRUNO is going to be a big hit, Mrs King. It's a wonderful new cereal!'

'What's in it?' asked Lucy.

'Crunchy wheat-flakes, rolled oats and succulent slivers of dried prune,' answered Mr Nutt with a beaming red-faced smile.

Lucy was horrified. She couldn't stand prunes. She loathed them. Mrs King knew exactly what poor Lucy was thinking and she whispered in her ear.

'I don't suppose you'll have to eat any, dear.

Just think, £2,000! Our first holiday for six years. It will only take a couple of minutes, I'm sure.'

Mrs King sounded as if she were calming Lucy before a visit to the dentist, but Lucy felt much worse than that. She sat back in the purring car thinking of slivers of dried prune. Her stomach gave an ominous grumble.

At the studio there were many more people than Lucy would have imagined necessary for making a film. There were cameramen, sound men, a director wearing an enormous tartan cloth cap, and lots of other people wandering around. A make-up lady spurted powder all over Lucy's face and put lipstick on her too.

'Right,' shouted the director, waving his arms above his head. 'Are we ready, everybody?' He looked at Lucy. 'Haven't you got your costume on yet?'

'What costume?' Lucy asked.

'Oh, come on! Time's money in this business, little girl. You lot always have costumes. Look at Batman and Robin. You know what I mean.'

Lucy had taken an instant dislike to the director. She looked helplessly at her mum.

'She doesn't have a costume,' murmured Mrs King. 'She does it as she is.'

The director practically exploded on the spot. 'What! Doesn't she twirl round and there's a flash and she re-appears in a flying suit or something?' Mrs King and Lucy both shook their heads.

'Why didn't anybody tell me this before!' screeched the director. 'Don't you even sprout wings?'

'No,' said Lucy, almost in tears.

'Oh, ruin!' cried the director, and he collapsed back in his chair. Luckily Mr Nutt came to the rescue.

'It really doesn't matter at all,' he said, beaming his big smile. 'All we want you to do is this. You come to the table and sit down for breakfast. You pour some PRUNO on to your plate and take a couple of mouthfuls. You look amazed at the wonderful taste and start rising up into the air as if it's PRUNO that has given you some special power. You go zooming through the ceiling.' Lucy looked up at the ceiling in alarm.

'Don't worry, it's made of strong paper. When you burst through the paper you'll find masses of PRUNO flakes up there and they'll come raining down on to the table, making a spectacular end to the advert. All right?' He beamed at Lucy.

She nodded and looked at the groaning director. Mr Nutt bent down and whispered to her.

'Don't worry about him. He's always like that. Take no notice.' Lucy smiled gratefully, and the filming went ahead.

Lucy walked up to the table and poured out her breakfast. She took a large spoonful of PRUNO and put it in her mouth, smiling at the whirring camera. She chewed the cereal for a moment and then suddenly turned green. Her eyes bulged, her nose shrivelled up and with a dreadful splutter she spat the offending cereal out. 'Urrrgh!' she cried, wiping her mouth vigorously.

'Cut!' screamed the director, tearing wildly at his hair. 'What do you think you're doing, you idiot?'

'It's horrible,' cried Lucy. 'I couldn't help it.'

'Really, Lucy,' said Mrs King lamely. Mr Nutt had hidden his face in his hands.

'You've ruined it!' shouted the director, leaping from his chair so that it went toppling backwards. He was almost berserk with rage.

'I told you I couldn't help it,' sobbed Lucy with tears in her eyes. 'I never did like prunes, and please don't shout at me like that.'

'Raaargh!' choked the director in his fury. He plucked his cloth cap from his head and hurled it at Lucy. She instinctively dodged the tartan missile by zooming up into the air.

She burst through the paper ceiling and a moment later the TV studio was rapidly disappearing beneath an endless downpour of PRUNO flakes. The camera crew tried to escape, crunching their way through the fallen flakes. One of them tripped over an electric cable. As he tried to stop himself falling, he accidentally switched on the wind-machine. A howling gale instantly turned the downpour into a whirling blizzard as PRUNO flakes whizzed round the studio, burying everything in sight.

Lucy crouched up amongst the rafters of the roof and watched with dismay. At last Mr Nutt managed to switch the wind-machine off and the flakes slowly settled. The studio floor was a deep sea of PRUNO. Parts of the sea stirred and crackled and heaved as people got back to their feet. The director was found sobbing quietly beneath a mound of soggy flakes.

'It's not fair!' he kept saying. 'I can't find my cap.'

Lucy drifted down from the rafters and joined

her mother. Mr Nutt sadly took them out to his
car. There was silence on the journey. It was not
until they reached the station that Mr Nutt
spoke. He tried to beam a smile at Lucy.

'It's not your fault,' he said kindly. 'I know
PRUNO is revolting. I can't stand it myself. Still,
you do realize we can't pay you?' Lucy nodded.

'Goodbye, Lucy,' said Mr Nutt, and he shook
her hand, turned and disappeared into the
crowd on the platform.

'Goodbye £2,000,' whispered Mrs King, but
Lucy heard her. She sat back in her seat on the
train and looked at her mother's tired face.

Tears welled up in her eyes and she couldn't
stop them from rolling down her cheeks, not
even with her special powers. It was all her fault.
No money, no holiday. She had spoiled things for
the whole family. The tears came faster and
faster.

Mrs King sat next to her daughter and put an
arm round her heaving shoulders. She was
dabbing at her own eyes with a little
handkerchief.

'Sssh,' sniffed Mrs King. 'It's not your fault,
Lucy. Forget all about it. I thought that director
was the most ill-mannered, horrible person I've

ever come across.' Mrs King gave a sudden laugh. 'He was even worse than Nicholas!' Lucy laughed a bit then, despite all her tears.

7 Thunder and Lightning Lucy

Lucy lay in bed with her head buried beneath her pillow.

'Do you think she's ill?' Mrs King asked her husband at the breakfast table. 'It's not like Lucy to lie in bed.'

'I know,' grunted Mr King. 'Usually she's up at 6 o'clock, waking everybody by leaping on them.' Mrs King tried to smile. Her husband continued. 'Leave her be. She's upset because of the advert failure.'

'I think we're all upset, Harold. What are we going to do? We put a £100 deposit on a holiday because we thought Lucy would get that advertisement money. Now we can't go on holiday after all. What will happen?'

Mr King stared glumly at the tablecloth. 'We shall just have to cancel the holiday,' he said in a flat voice.

'But what will happen to our £100 deposit?'

Mr King answered her bluntly. 'Oh, we'll lose that. Gone. Nothing we can do about it.'

A long silence filled the room. Mr and Mrs King tried not to look at each other. They didn't want to see the dismay they both felt. At last Mr King spoke. He reached out one hand and laid it over his wife's hands.

'This is what we'll do. We shall go up to the High Street this morning and cancel the holiday. It's cattle-market day so the kids can watch that, while we do the worst bit. Then we'll go to that little cafe near the market and have a bite to eat. In the afternoon we'll all go to the cinema and forget our worries. The kids will like the pictures.'

Mrs King thought it was a splendid idea and when Lucy heard the news she jumped out of bed immediately. Nicholas was excited too.

'What's on at the cinema, Dad?' asked Lucy, already full of energy.

'I bet it's a real scary film,' hinted Nicholas. 'I

expect Lucy will hide under her seat. Did you know that she's afraid of cabbage?'

'I'm not!' yelled Lucy indignantly. 'You're an idiot.'

'You are. You're afraid of cabbage because the last time we had cabbage at school you put your hands over your face and started trembling.'

'All right, all right, break it up,' said Dad. 'I'll tell you what's on. It's a film called *Lightning Never Strikes Twice*. It's an adventure film about some jewel thieves or something.'

'Great!' said both kids, agreeing with each other for once.

The family decided to walk up to the High Street since it wasn't too far. Mum glanced out of the window before they left. 'Coats on, everybody,' she said. 'It looks like rain.'

The clouds were building up heavily. They glowered above, purple and angry, making the street quite dark.

'The weather is as gloomy as I feel,' murmured Mr King to his wife.

'I feel the same,' she said. 'Never mind, Lucy and Nicholas have cheered up.'

They left the two children at the market and went on ahead to the travel agent, where they waited sadly at the counter to be attended to. The travel agent said he was sorry they were cancelling their holiday.

'You do realize,' he continued, 'that you will lose your £100 deposit?' Mr King just nodded. His wife put one arm through his, and pulled him away from the counter.

'Come on,' she said, trying to sound cheerful. 'Let's grab a cup of coffee.'

When they got outside it seemed darker than ever. Down at the market Lucy and Nicholas were having a good time. Lucy had quite forgotten about the disaster at the TV studio, and was running around madly, with Nicholas close at her heels.

'Look at those turkeys,' shouted Nicholas, pointing at a turkey-pen. 'They look as if they've just spilt rhubarb tart down their fronts.'

Then they climbed up some railings and peered over at three enormous white pigs, snuffling around in the straw.

'Help!' cried Lucy suddenly.

'What's up?' asked Nicholas in alarm.

'A pig's escaped!' Two nearby farmers stared all around. So did Nicholas.

'Where?' he cried. 'Where is it?'

'There!' shouted Lucy, pointing straight at her brother. He groaned.

'I suppose you think that's funny.' The two farmers were nudging each other and smiling. Nicholas tried to change the subject.

'Do you think it's going to rain? It's awfully dark.' Lucy glanced at the massing clouds. There was a rumble of thunder in the distance and a flash of lightning. The children looked for Mr and Mrs King. They weren't afraid of the approaching storm, but they didn't want to get wet.

Nicholas spotted them at the far side of the market and they ran over to join them, just as the first spots of rain began to fall. The cattle began to moo noisily. The thunder and lightning made them restless. They flicked their tails irritably and banged against the sides of their pens.

There was a sudden, blinding flash of lightning that slammed down on the market, followed immediately by a deafening explosion across the sky. The market animals exploded in their own chaotic way. Hens squawked and flapped, sending puffs of feathers up in the air. Sheep bleated and charged round their pens.

The cattle bellowed and banged against their railings, which rocked furiously. Another hiss of lightning overhead made the cows charge at the railings again, and this time the sides of the pen fell away. Suddenly there were cows all over the market.

Kicking their frightened heels and mooing at the tops of their lungs, the lumbering beasts thundered out of the market and clattered up the High Street. Behind them came a long trail of puffing, shouting and waving farmers.

The storm got under way. The rain fell like bullets, bouncing from the hard road. Both cows and farmers were soaked. Lightning flickered continuously, as if a giant fuse in the sky had just blown. It became impossible to tell when one clatter of thunder finished and the next started.

The cows careered up the High Street, swerved round cars and scattered shoppers. Women screamed as they dragged their children to safety. Drivers hooted and skidded and crashed into lamp posts, into each other and into shopfronts, as they desperately tried to avoid being trampled by the galloping beasts. Some of the cattle appeared to get bored with the High

Street. They lurched to one side and dashed into a supermarket.

Till operators screamed and ran into the manager's office. The manager came running out, shouting and waving a newspaper. The cows took no notice. They were far too busy doing their shopping. They cannoned into displays of tins. They squashed great mounds of fruit beneath their clumping hooves. They skidded on the soggy mess they had just made and sat on the potted plants. Then they played bumper cars with the shopping trolleys, sending them crashing into each other. The cows bellowed and charged back into the High Street.

'Go away,' moaned the manager as he collapsed into a shopping trolley.

The High Street was in chaos. The cattle were thundering everywhere, trying to get into the smallest shops. Above the sound of the storm came the hubbub of shouts and breaking glass, mooing and snapping wood.

When Lucy saw the High Street, she could not stop herself from acting. Her hair crackled with a shower of sparks. The red glow shimmered round her body. She stood for a moment letting her powers fill right up and then she took to the air and zoomed over amazed heads.

At the top of the High Street there was a statue of some famous townsman. Lucy swooped down and landed upon the statue's shoulders. She faced the stampeding cattle and spread her arms in front, fingers outstretched. Her fiery halo grew stronger until it seemed like leaping flames. The redness streamed from her fingertips towards the galloping cattle.

One by one they slowed down as they felt Lucy's awesome power tightening round them like an unseen rope. But there were too many of the creatures. Despite her power, Lucy was frightened.

The frenzied cows were all over the place. Lucy tried to send her gathering rays around them, casting the rays like a net. The distance was too great and the cattle too many. She began to feel her powers draining fast. The red glow started to flicker and fade. Her legs got wobbly and Lucy had to clutch at the statue with fumbling fingers to stop herself from falling. All at once Lucy knew she was going to faint.

An ear-splitting crack of thunder burst above her dizzy head and a bolt of lightning whammed down from the black sky. It struck Lucy from head to toe. The crowd fell back, half-blinded by the intense glare. There was a hissing, sizzling noise and a crack split the statue in two, but it didn't collapse. Lucy stood transfixed by the lightning – it was a sight that everybody remembered for years afterwards. She glowed the most radiant red ever. Great cascades of shimmering sparks leaped from both Lucy and the statue.

The lightning died and Lucy zoomed into the air leaving a trail of glorious sparks behind. She dived and climbed and swooped between lamp posts, rounding up the cattle and bringing them into a huddle round the smoking statue. Then, with a broad grin on her smudgy face, she drove the timid beasts back down the High Street and into the market, to be sorted out by the farmers. The cattle behaved like little lambs. Only then did Lucy idly fly back to her parents and Nicholas.

'I could do with a cup of tea,' she said, wiping the hair from her eyes.

But the town would not let Lucy have a cup of tea. The whole family was surrounded by cheering shopkeepers and shoppers. They all wished to thank Lucy for saving the town from further damage. One man pushed his way to the front of the crowd. It was the travel agent.

'Is this your daughter?' he shouted at Mr and Mrs King. 'She was fantastic – and that lightning! It was incredible. I've never seen anything like it in my life. Lightning Lucy – that's what we ought to call her. Do you know Lightning Lucy just made two cows leave my shop? I thought they were going to eat all my aeroplane tickets.' He turned excitedly to Mr King. 'She saved my shop, you know. I'm really very grateful. Look, about that deposit. Forget about it, please. Just go ahead as planned.' Mr King looked at the travel agent with open mouth.

'What do you mean?' he stammered.

'Take the holiday!' cried the travel agent. 'Just go ahead as planned. How long were you going for?'

'Two weeks,' answered Mr King, in quite a daze.

'Make it four!' cried the travel agent happily. 'Don't worry about a thing. Your daughter has saved me far more than a holiday will cost.'

And so it was. Two months later, the King

family were sitting on an aeroplane, flying to Greece, on a four-week holiday.

'I still find it hard to believe,' said Mr King.

'Lightning Lucy,' murmured Mrs King. 'It's a good name. She's just like a thunderstorm at home, what with her noise and mess and everything.'

'Let's just hope there are no thunderstorms in Greece,' grinned Mr King. He glanced at Lucy and Nicholas.

Nicholas was sitting back, staring out of the window and thoroughly enjoying his first flight. Leaning against his shoulder was his sister, fast asleep. Flying was nothing new to Lightning Lucy.

Lightning Lucy
Strikes Again

1 Identified Flying Objects

When Lucy King was just six months old her pram was struck by lightning. As she was fast asleep inside it at the time, her parents were terribly worried. They rushed out to her and were astonished to discover that she was quite unharmed. In fact, she was lying in her pram and gurgling with laughter, whilst the pram itself had a faint red glow all around it, from the huge shock of electricity that had passed through it.

Of course Mr and Mrs King thought their daughter had had a miraculous escape and eventually they almost forgot about it. But as she grew up Lucy began to behave rather oddly.

When she was four she fell into the goldfish pond. Before her startled parents could rush to her aid, Lucy had zoomed out of the pond and flown – flown! – up to the safety of the apple tree.

At the age of seven she rescued her younger brother, Nicholas, from certain death. A truck was about to run him over. Lucy flew across the road and swept him up out of harm's way.

Mr and Mrs King had to accept that their daughter could fly. Then Lucy discovered that if she thought hard enough about an object she could make *that* fly too. So she thought very hard about Nicholas and made him fly through the air and then land upside down on top of her wardrobe. Neither Mum nor Nicholas had been very pleased about that, but Lucy was delighted.

The trouble was that Lucy was a bit of a scatterbrain and although she seemed to have the most marvellous powers they got her into as many awkward spots as good ones. However, one stormy afternoon she had managed to stop a whole herd of cows stampeding through the town centre, whilst amazed shoppers watched. It was then that she became known as 'Lightning Lucy'.

A grateful shop owner even offered the Kings a free holiday in Greece as a reward for saving his shop from being wrecked by rampaging cows. The Kings were not very rich and it was a marvellous opportunity. So, thanks to Lucy, the whole family went off to Greece for four weeks.

They had a wonderful time. They swam and sunbathed and saw all the sights. They danced themselves silly at the discos and ate strange food. Nicholas found a baby octopus when he went diving and wanted to bring it home, but Mum wouldn't let him. The only time Lucy had to use her special power was when Nicholas fell over the balcony rail. She whizzed down in a shower of sparks and grabbed him before he hit the ground. She was getting used to that sort of thing.

Now it was their last day in Greece, and Lucy was gazing fondly round the little bedroom that had been home for the last four weeks.

'I don't want to go home,' she murmured. 'I shall have to start piano practice again.'

'And we shall have to go back to school,' said Nicholas. 'Why don't we stay behind?'

'How can we do that?'

'Easy. We could hide inside a cupboard or something.'

'Don't be daft,' said Lucy. 'Mum and Dad would look for you. They'd soon find you.'

'I'll hide somewhere they can't find me,' insisted Nicholas.

'They won't go without you.'

Nicholas grinned. 'In that case we shall all have to stay behind!' He crumpled up his last pair of shorts, rammed them into his suitcase and sat on the lid. Lucy went to the balcony and stared out across the blue sea. She sighed.

'Come on. Let's go downstairs. Mum and Dad will be waiting at our table. They said it will be special tonight because it's our last proper meal in Greece.'

'Race you!' yelled Nicholas, hastily adding, 'and you're not allowed to fly. That's cheating.' He skidded out of the room and went pounding downstairs two at a time. Lucy was right behind him. Together they burst into the dining room and thundered across to their table.

'Please, please!' cried Mrs King. 'Don't come into the dining room like that.'

'We were having a race,' panted Nicholas. 'I won.'

'No you didn't!' shouted Lucy. 'I sat down before you.'

'But I got to the dining room before you,' cried Nicholas.

'And I shall send you both back upstairs if you can't behave properly,' interrupted Dad. He glared at them for a few moments, daring them to speak. Then he smiled. 'Well, our last meal. Why don't we have a bottle of champagne to celebrate our holiday?'

'Champagne!' Lucy cried.

'Fantastic!' said Nicholas, his eyes as big as wine glasses.

Mrs King touched her husband's arm gently. 'Are you sure we can afford it, dear?' He grinned at her and winked.

'It's not proper French champagne. It's just fizzy wine really, but I don't suppose we shall notice the difference. We don't get much practice at sipping champagne, do we?'

Mrs King was still looking a little concerned. 'What about the children? Do you think it's all right for them?'

'Of course it is. One glass won't do them any harm.' Mr King nudged his wife. 'It's me you've got to worry about. Too much champagne and I go all bubbly myself!'

Mrs King laughed. 'The sooner we all get home, the better. Maybe things will be normal then, though how anything can ever be normal with Lucy around, I don't know. Ah! Here comes the waiter.'

It wasn't long before they were all eating away at platefuls of food. The bottle of champagne arrived, nestling in a big bucket of ice. Lucy and Nicholas were delighted when the waiter popped the cork so that it flew across the room, bounced off the ceiling and almost ended up in somebody's soup.

The waiter poured out four glasses of champagne. Then the bubbles in the drink got up Nicholas's nose and he sneezed. Everybody in the dining room turned to see what was going on.

'That sneeze sounded like another cork going off,' said Lucy with a little giggle.

'I don't think it was that funny,' said Mum, but the bubbles began to work on her and she started smiling too.

After twenty minutes all the Kings were getting giggly. Lucy finished her glass of champagne and Mr King poured out a second glass for her.

'Do you think that's wise, Harold?' Mrs King asked her husband.

'It is our last day,' Mr King pointed out.

Lucy's eyes popped with delight and she took a huge sip.

The waiter came and cleared their plates. He took their orders for pudding. Nicholas watched him hurry back to the kitchen.

'I'm glad I'm not a waiter,' he said. 'They have to do so much rushing backwards and forwards. Kitchen to table to kitchen to table . . . I'm glad I'm not one.'

'What – a table?' asked Lucy.

'No, you stupid dustbrain!'

'Well, are you glad you're not a kitchen then?'

'No!'

'That's what you said. You said that you were glad you weren't . . .'

'All right, Lucy,' Dad interrupted. 'That's enough.'

Lucy grinned at Nicholas and whispered to him, 'I know what I'd do if I were a waiter. I wouldn't keep rushing around like a mad penguin.'

'What would you do?' asked Nicholas.

'I'd make all the tables come to me. I'd make them rise up in the air and come to me.'

'You couldn't do that, could you?'

'Of course I could.' Lucy began to giggle once

more. 'It would be easy.' She watched a waiter hurry to a table and then back to the kitchen. Another waiter burst out from the kitchen, with plates of food in both hands.

There was a startled cry from the far end of the dining room. A chair toppled over, throwing a fat old holiday-maker to the floor. Everybody stared across at the far corner. One of the huge round dining tables was rising up in the air. It hovered overhead and slowly began to revolve. Then it skimmed across the room with its tablecloth gently flapping, just below the ceiling. The waiter went plunging after it with his plates of food.

Nicholas was falling off his chair with the giggles. 'It's an unidentified flying table!' he crowed. Lucy sat very quietly with a faint red glow all around her and a distant look in her twinkling eyes. Mum and Dad guessed exactly what was going on.

'Lucy!' hissed Dad. 'Lucy, stop it! Put that table down at once!'

But Lucy was in a trance of concentration and the table went on travelling round the room, with the waiter stumbling after it, puffing and panting and desperate to put his hot plates down.

Mum leaned across the table and seized Lucy
by the arm.

'Stop it, Lucy!' Mum shook her daughter
violently. The floating table lurched sideways
and everything slid off and rained down on the
tables beneath – plates, cups, food, glasses,
knives, forks – everything. Then the table went
into a nose-dive and crashed to the floor, where
it lay on one side, rolling drunkenly.

'Oh, Lucy!' wailed Mum. Lucy shook out her
crackling curls and started giggling.

'It wasn't my fault. If you hadn't disturbed me
it would have landed perfectly.'

'I doubt it,' said Dad. 'Anyway, it's certainly
nothing to laugh about.' He watched the waiters
clearing up the mess. The dining room was
buzzing with excited chatter as the diners
wondered how it had all happened. It was an
amazing mystery, except to the Kings.

Nicholas began laughing again, and that
made Lucy start up.

'Unidentified flying tables!' he spluttered
again.

'Intergalactic soup bowls!' hooted Lucy.

Mr and Mrs King stood up. They glanced at
each other and nodded. 'I think it might be a

good idea to get these two up to bed,' said Mum. 'Something tells me they've had a little bit too much to drink.' She sighed. 'The sooner we get back home, the better.'

But even as she said it she knew that no matter where they were, Lucy would always be Lightning Lucy and there would be storms wherever she went.

2 Lost Luggage

The first thing that happened to the Kings when they arrived at the airport back in England was that their luggage got lost. They searched and searched, but couldn't see it anywhere.

'It's like looking for a needle in a haystack,' grumbled Mr King, as he stared around at the great mounds of cases and bags and trunks and rucksacks that kept on being unloaded from the arriving planes.

'Are you sure you labelled them properly?' asked Mrs King.

'Of course I did!' snapped Dad.

'Maybe they've been sent to another country,' Lucy suggested.

'And we shall have to go there to get them

back,' added Nicholas, with a sly smile.

Mr King paced angrily up and down. 'There must be thousands of cases here,' he declared. 'It's no good – I shall have to go and search the whole airport. You stay here and keep an eye on this moving luggage belt, just in case it comes through that way. I'll have a look around and see if I can get anybody to help.'

He strode off and soon vanished among the crowds of people who were bustling about, pushing and shoving and shouting at each other in twenty different languages.

Nicholas climbed up the barrier that separated them from the moving luggage belt, and sat astride it. It was fascinating watching the luggage come through: tartan bags, brown bags, blue bags, leather suitcases and strangely shaped packages – all too big to go in the luggage racks of the plane.

Mrs King kept standing on tiptoe, to see over the heads of the seething crowd. She was hoping to spot her husband. She glanced anxiously at her watch as time went by and told Lucy she was afraid Dad had got himself lost.

'I'll go and look for him,' offered Lucy, but Mum grabbed her by the collar before Lucy could disappear into the crowd as well.

'You stay here,' said Mum. 'I don't want both of you lost. We shall do far better waiting together.'

Lucy joined Nicholas at the barrier. He pointed to the end of the luggage belt, rumbling away on the other side.

'Look,' he said, 'you can see where all the cases get sorted into a single line. Then that machine at the side weighs each case and the big blue thing above comes down and stamps a label on it and it disappears down that little tunnel. I suppose it goes to the plane after that.'

Lucy watched all the luggage being sorted, weighed and stamped. It was almost hypnotic. She saw the baggage vanish down the tunnel, and an odd thought came to her.

'Nicholas,' she said, 'if all that luggage is being stamped to go on the aeroplanes, why are we waiting here to try and find ours? Our luggage should be coming off the plane, not going on to it.'

Nicholas's jaw dropped open and he gazed at his sister for several seconds. 'You'd better tell Mum,' he whispered. Lucy told Mum and Mum smiled and told them not to be silly. Dad knew what he was doing.

'He can't possibly have made us wait all this time in the wrong place,' she said. 'Just keep an eye on that luggage belt.' Then she had a quick glance round to see if there were any signs to show that they were waiting in the wrong place.

Suddenly several things happened at once. Mr King came hurrying out of the crowd, shouting and waving. At the same time a huge, fat old gentleman bustled up against Nicholas and knocked him from his perch on the barrier. He landed head first among the moving suitcases and bags. For a moment he was dazed. Then he struggled to the surface and shouted.

'Help!'

The Kings turned to stare. They were just in time to see Nicholas being weighed. Then he was under the blue machine and a label was being stuck on top of his head.

'Do something, Harold!' wailed Mrs King.

'Stop the luggage belt!' yelled Mr King.

'Ouch!' cried Nicholas, trying to peel the label off his head, whilst the tunnel that led to the departing planes came closer and closer, a huge black mouth ready to gobble Nicholas up and make him disappear for ever, probably to Peru or Tibet or somewhere like that.

Suddenly, there was a fizz of sparks and Lucy leaped into action. Down she darted at lightning speed, grabbed her brother's arm and pulled him from the mouth of the tunnel. She sped back to Mum and Dad and plonked Nicholas down beside them. Then she shook her mass of red curls and tiny red sparks glittered as they fell to the floor.

'Honestly, Nicholas,' she complained, 'I'm getting fed up with rescuing you. I wish you'd learn to fly for yourself.'

The other travellers were nudging each other and pointing at Lucy.

'Did you see that? She flew through the air!'

'She saved that little boy's life!'

'. . . just like Superman, and she was glowing all over . . .'

Mr King hustled his family along in front of him. This was the last thing he wanted. He hated it when everybody saw Lucy's amazing powers. He knew it wasn't her fault, and her powers were often very useful, but he didn't like all the attention it brought them. They had gone away on holiday to escape all the attention. Now, the moment they were back in England Lucy was zooming around and they were the centre of attraction once again.

'Come on,' he muttered. 'Keep moving. Let's get out of here before somebody starts asking questions and they find out who you are. They'll only want photographs and autographs and everything.'

'What about the luggage?' asked Mrs King.

'I've found that. You were waiting in the wrong place. That was where the luggage was being put on the plane.'

'See? I told you, Mum,' said Lucy.

'And I told you,' butted in Nicholas. 'I noticed it first.'

'You didn't! All you said was . . .'

'I did, I did! You always pinch my ideas. Just because you can fly you think you're brilliant but . . .'

'Shut up!' yelled Dad. The whole airport froze and turned to stare at Mr King, rapidly turning a very embarrassed purple colour. 'Will you two stop quarrelling for one minute?' he hissed. 'Here's the luggage. Everybody take a case each and if you two say another word again I'll, I'll, I'll . . . put Nicholas and Lucy back on the luggage belt. Then maybe we'll get a bit of peace!'

They managed to get outside the airport

without any more wars. Mr King called a taxi
and it wasn't very long before they were pulling
up outside their own home.

They hardly recognized it. The house was
covered in coloured streamers and little flags.
There was a sheet hanging from two upstairs
windows, with large red letters sprawled across
it:

WELCOME HOME LIGHTNING LUCY OUR HEROINE!!

Lucy jumped out of the taxi and stared.
'Wow!' she breathed. Nicholas slumped back in
his seat and muttered something about his
sister's head getting too big for her to get
through their front door any longer.

'Come on,' coaxed Mum. 'Give us a hand
with the luggage. Lucy can't help being special,
you know. We're really quite lucky to have such a
clever girl in the family.' Then Mum bent down
close and whispered into Nicholas's left ear,
'Only don't ever tell Lucy that, or she *will* get
big-headed!' Nicholas laughed and grabbed one
of the cases.

The neighbours were very kind. They had

prepared a special tea for all the family, and the Kings felt rather proud and a bit embarrassed.

'You shouldn't have gone to all this trouble,' murmured Mrs King.

'Nonsense,' cried Mr Jackson from across the road. 'It's not every street that has a real superhero – I mean, superheroine – living in it. We're all jolly pleased. I always thought Lucy was a lovely girl.'

Lucy overheard this last remark and wondered why Mr Jackson had been so rude to her a couple of months earlier if he thought she was a lovely girl. After all, it wasn't her fault that his dog had been so scared by her zooming across the park that it had jumped into the duck pond.

Mr and Mrs King were very pleased when the tea party was over and everybody was able to go back to their homes. They took down the bunting and the sheet hanging out of the upstairs windows. Then they set about putting things straight after their four-week holiday.

They unpacked the suitcases and sorted out the dirty washing and put all their souvenirs out on display. Nicholas seemed to have brought back nothing but bits of rock.

'What do you want those for?' demanded Lucy.

'When I have a bath I'm going to stick them in the middle, and then I shall have my own Greek island,' he explained.

'Call the doctor, Mum,' sighed Lucy. 'Nick's gone potty.'

Mum wagged a finger at Lucy. 'Don't call him Nick. It sounds terrible. He's got a proper name, so use it.'

Nicholas looked up from arranging his rocks. 'I don't mind being called Nick. I like it.'

'Don't argue,' snapped Mum. Nicholas glanced at Lucy and shrugged.

Mrs King made a cup of tea while Mr King made sure the children had a good bath before he settled them in bed. At length he came downstairs quietly and flopped into an armchair. Mrs King passed him his tea.

'There are three sacks of letters waiting for Lucy to open,' she said. Mr King groaned.

'Oh no, I thought we might have said goodbye to all that. I was hoping people would have forgotten about her by now. Will we never get any peace? Why can't we just live ordinary lives, like everybody else? It can't go on. It will drive us mad.'

Mrs King nodded. 'What can we do?' she asked.

Mr King rubbed his forehead and took several sips from his tea. At length he looked up at his wife. 'We could always go and live somewhere else,' he said. 'Yes – we could move house.'

3 The Football Tournament

Lucy was not very fond of school. Her teacher, Mr Barber, was all right. He was quite kind really, and only shouted at her about five times every day. Lucy thought this wasn't too bad because her friend Robert got shouted at about twenty times a day.

The problem was that Lucy didn't like work at all, and just recently she had begun to spend all her time thinking about football and nothing else. It was her latest passion.

Robert was in the school team and Lucy played football with him and his friends every playtime. They all thought she was pretty good. When she got home, Lucy would pester Mrs King to fit her out with the colours of her favourite team, but since Lucy changed her favourite team every week Mrs King decided it wasn't worth it.

One morning at assembly, Mrs Conway, the head teacher, told the school that there was going to be a football tournament for the local schools. Their school would take part, as usual. They had won the tournament for the last two years, and if they won it again this year, it would be a hat-trick and they would be allowed to keep the big silver trophy for ever. Usually the trophy was kept by the winners just for the year and then handed over to the new winners.

Mrs Conway pointed out that the school team had been playing very well this season and had won most of their matches.

'However,' she continued, 'we must not get big-headed about it. There are one or two tough teams that we shall have to beat. Downsland School will be taking part and I hear that their team is very strong this year. Well, the tournament takes place this weekend, so let's wish our team the best of luck.'

After assembly, Lucy spoke to Robert.

'I wish I was playing. Are you going to be in the team, Robert?'

'Probably. I don't fancy playing the Downsland team though.'

'Are they really good?'

Robert gave a hollow laugh. 'They're no good at all. They foul all the time. They trip you up and kick and push, but somehow the ref never notices. I bet you we have to play them in the final – if we make it that far!'

Lucy clapped him on the shoulders. 'Of course you'll make it to the final! You're brilliant!'

'I wish you were playing for us,' said Robert. Lucy's face went glum all over.

'Fat chance,' she muttered.

Then awful things began to happen to the football team. The right-wing got chickenpox. Their star goal scorer tripped over his new puppy at home and fell and broke his arm. To make matters worse, even the school's amazing goalkeeper (nicknamed 'Octopus' because his hands were all over the goal mouth) knocked himself out on a goal post during training. He was carried off to hospital and was told to stay there for two days. That meant he would miss the tournament.

Mr Barber, who looked after the football

team, was going frantic. He had already used his reserves filling the first two places. He searched all the classes for signs of a good new goalkeeper, but there was no one.

The day before the tournament Mr Barber sat moodily at his desk, wondering what to do. Robert took up his work book to be checked. Mr Barber was so deep in thought he didn't even notice.

Robert waited and eventually coughed loudly. Mr Barber gave a startled jump, but instead of being cross he mumbled an apology.

'Sorry, Robert. I was just trying to figure out what to do with the football team tomorrow. Three of our best players won't be there and I can't find anybody to replace Octopus. I'm afraid we're going to lose that cup.' Mr Barber heaved a sigh and continued to stare blankly into space.

Robert nodded slowly. 'Why don't you try Lucy King, Mr Barber? She often plays with us at playtime and she's ex.'

'Ex?' repeated Mr Barber. 'What's ex?'

'Ex! You know – excellent, ace, brill!'

Mr Barber frowned and looked across at Lucy. She was leaning far back on her chair, as usual, and talking noisily to the girl behind her. He could see she hadn't done a stroke of work all morning. He groaned to himself.

'She *is* good, Mr Barber,' said Robert once more. Mr Barber nodded reluctantly. He didn't have much choice.

'All right, I'll have a word with her. Lucy!' There was a loud clatter as Lucy fell off her chair in guilty surprise. The class began to laugh and Lucy clambered out from the wreckage.

'All right, class,' said Mr Barber. 'Get on with your work. Lucy, I want a word with you.'

When Lucy discovered that Mr Barber wanted to try her out as goalkeeper in the team she was over the moon. She went home walking on air, which made a change from flying through it. She was so excited that she dreamed all night about scoring six million goals, all with her left foot.

At the weekend the whole family turned up for the football tournament. There were about ten schools taking part. The first three matches were fairly easy and Lucy had little work to do. She only let in one goal and the rest of the team played well and scored quite a few. They got through to the semi-final.

'Do your best,' Mr Barber told them, quite unnecessarily. 'Downsland are playing in the other semi-final. Let's hope they don't make it.'

The semi-final was a tough match. The other team were good and Lucy let in three goals. This upset her and she felt useless.

'Don't give up,' shouted Robert, racing upfield after the ball.

'But I've let in three,' Lucy wailed.

'And you've saved hundreds!' he pointed out.

In the end Lucy's school won 5−4. It had been too close for Lucy's liking. To make matters worse, Downsland won their match 9−1. It was a taste of things to come. Lucy felt like giving up on the spot. The rest of the team were pretty downcast too. Some of them had played Downsland before.

They had a half-hour break before the final to get their strength back. Then it was back on to the pitch.

Mr and Mrs King and Nicholas stood on the touchline, cheering their heads off. The referee blew the whistle and the match started. Downsland were on to the ball straight away. Their star player was about two metres tall and built like a gorilla – or so he seemed to Lucy as he charged towards her with the ball at his feet. He slammed it straight at her and she had the breath knocked clean from her body in saving it.

'Well done, Lucy!' yelled Mr King. The Downsland Gorilla stood over her.

'Lucy?' he snarled. 'Lucy?' He turned upfield and bellowed, 'Hey – their goalie's a girl! She's a girl!' He ran upfield punching his fist in the air and yelling, 'We'll massacre them! Girlies! Girlies!'

Lucy got her breath back and kicked the ball upfield. Her eyes blazed. If only she could use her power to lift that great stinking gorilla into the air and drop him off somewhere nice, like the nearby duck pond. Her hair crackled with electricity and she stretched out her fingers. There was a sharp voice behind her.

'Don't do it,' warned Mr Barber, who knew all about Lucy's special tricks. 'You'll get the whole team disqualified.'

Lucy lowered her arms helplessly. She watched the tussle for the ball going on, then Downsland came thundering back. The defence went sprawling in the mud. They couldn't get near the ball. The Downsland Gorilla loomed into view and pounded the ball into the net.

After that it went on and on. Downsland kept
coming back and every time Lucy's team tried to
tackle they ended up crashing to the ground.
Soon two of the team had been taken off with
twisted ankles and bruised shins and there was
nobody to replace them. They complained about
the fouling but the ref seemed to be deaf – not to
mention blind.

Poor Lucy couldn't keep up with the relentless
attack. Downsland would come right up to the
goal mouth before they even took a kick. They
could hardly miss. When the first half finished,
the score was 7–2 to Downsland, and Lucy's
team only had eight players left.

Mr and Mrs King tried to cheer the team up,
especially Lucy, who felt she was letting her side
down dreadfully. Nicholas wanted Lucy to make
the whole Downsland team float away to the top
of Mount Everest but Mr King said why spoil
Mount Everest? It hadn't done any harm.

That cheered the team up a little and they
went back on to the pitch determined to do their
best. But Lucy was still thoroughly fed up. It just
wasn't a fair match. She really wanted to use her
powers but she knew that if anybody saw, then
the team would be disqualified. It was not until

the Downsland Gorilla scored an eighth goal and called her 'Girly!' for the hundredth time that she began to have an idea.

The next time she kicked the ball upfield she gave it a little extra help. The ball turned very faintly red and not only travelled twice as far but landed beautifully, right at the feet of their centre half. He leaped on the ball, whisked it forward and scored from a powering long shot.

Lucy did that several more times, until Mr Barber came and stood behind the goal and watched her closely, with a severe frown on his face. Lucy wondered if he wasn't smiling just a little too. Anyhow, he couldn't see what she was doing because she didn't even need to point her fingers as the ball was so light.

Then Downsland got the ball once more and came stampeding back down the pitch. Lucy smiled to herself and waited. The Downsland Gorilla took an almighty swipe at the ball, but somehow the ball wasn't there any longer. It had sort of moved sideways. The Gorilla kicked the empty air and fell flat on his back in the mud. Lucy grabbed the ball, kicked it upfield and placed it just right for a goal.

Now every time Downsland got near Lucy's

goal strange things happened. The ball would hop sideways or jump up and bonk the Downsland players on the head. Sometimes a shot would come straight at the goal and stop dead, as if it had hit an invisible force, which of course it had. Lucy leaned against a goal post, with her hair sticking out a bit more than usual.

Gradually the score changed and the Downsland players became more and more furious. When the Gorilla fell over for the sixth time after trying to kick a ball that wasn't there, Lucy called out to him, 'Would you like a hand getting up? I'm only a girl, but you seem a little wobbly on your pegs today!' The Downsland Gorilla struggled up, plucked a huge clod of mud from his hair and hurled it at her. It missed of course.

When the final whistle went, the score was 11−9 to Lucy's team. She was carried shoulder-high round the pitch, while Mr and Mrs King talked quietly with Mr Barber.

'Strange match, wasn't it?' said Mr Barber, with a ghost of a smile. 'Did you see Lucy do anything, because I didn't.'

Mr King grinned. 'I didn't see Lucy do anything, but I saw the ball do the most extraordinary things. Do you know, it almost made me think that ball had special powers!'

All three of them shook their heads and laughed, while the victorious team collected the silver trophy. It was theirs to keep.

4 Lucy Plays with Fire

Being a member of a triumphant football team did a lot for Lucy. She did everything a little better. Her school work was neater and she didn't fall off her chair quite so often.

'It's a miracle,' said Mr Barber. 'Let's just hope it lasts.'

Lucy played for the team regularly and it kept her busy all through the winter. She was quite sorry when the football season ended.

'I wish we could play all year round,' she confided to Robert.

'I'm going to try and get in the cricket team,' Robert said. 'Why don't you?'

'Cricket! What do you want to play that game for? All you do is stand in the middle of a field all day long. You might as well decide to be a cow.'

'Mooo!' teased Robert, and he went off to practise his bowling.

Once more Lucy was left with nothing to do. She began to lose interest in other things and soon her work had slipped back into the untidy mess it had been before.

'I knew it couldn't last,' sighed Mr Barber, all to himself.

One day, when Lucy and Nicholas got home from school, Mrs King had news for them. They had managed to sell the house, and in a couple of months they would be moving.

'But where are we going?' asked Lucy.

'Back to Greece?' suggested Nicholas hopefully.

'I'm afraid Greece will have to wait until we win lots of money,' smiled Mrs King. 'But do you remember that house we went to look at last month – the one with the long garden and the swing? We're going to move there. It's not too far, so you won't have to change school. We simply must get away from here. Every day there seem to be more callers wanting Lucy's autograph or wanting her to do something special for them. Your father and I don't get a moment's peace.'

Lucy and Nicholas looked glum. They didn't want to move at all. They had spent all their lives in the same house. It didn't seem possible to change anything now.

'What about my bedroom and everything?' Lucy asked.

'You'll have a new bedroom. You can choose some wallpaper for it if you like.'

Lucy brightened up. 'Can I have that one with the motorbikes roaring across doing wheelies and things?'

Mrs King winced. 'I hardly think that's suitable for your bedroom, Lucy.'

'Oh, Mum!'

'I should think the noise of the bikes would keep you awake all night. Can't you think of something a bit more peaceful?'

Lucy thought. 'There's quite a good one with Indians about to ambush the United States Cavalry, and the captain or general or whatever has got a spear in his back and he's falling off his horse with blood drip—'

'Lucy! You are not going to have wallpaper with blood dripping from it. Now, please! Let's forget about wallpaper for a moment.'

Lucy wandered aimlessly around the kitchen a few times and then asked what they'd got for tea.

'Liver,' replied Mrs King, and before Lucy could say a thing, she added, 'Don't say a word and don't pull any faces. Liver is very good for you. There's lots of iron in liver.'

'Iron!' cried Lucy. 'I shall go rusty all over. I'll get horrible brown blotches and my arms and legs will fall off!'

Mrs King pointed silently at the kitchen door. She didn't want to hear any more. Lucy grunted and went out. As she reached the door, Mrs King called after her, 'You'd better do your piano practice.'

Lucy stopped dead, as if she had just been speared by a wallpaper Indian. 'Oh, Mum!'

'Piano practice.'

Lucy stamped off to the front room, trying to make up her mind which was worse – piano practice or liver. She sat down at the keyboard and began to play her scales very slowly.

'Do them properly!' yelled Mum from the kitchen. Lucy played so fast her fingers tripped over each other.

'Do them properly!'

Lucy stopped and thought. There must be something she could do to make piano practice more interesting. She took the piano stool away and tried floating in the air while she thumped out her scales. First she tried floating cross-legged and then she spread out flat, as if she were lying on a bed. It was certainly a lot more fun playing the piano like this. She tried standing upside down, so that her feet were resting on the ceiling.

Nicholas came in and watched her. 'Your face has gone red,' he said. 'All the blood's run to your head. I don't suppose there's any left in your feet. Can I do it too?' Lucy lifted one hand from the piano and pointed at Nicholas. He began to rise slowly from the carpet. Lucy turned him upside down so that they were side by side.

'Do you fancy a walk?' asked Lucy. Nicholas grinned. They held hands and began to walk round the ceiling. 'It's an interesting view, isn't it?' said Lucy, as they hovered over the settee.

The door opened and Mum came in. 'Come down at once! I wondered how those muddy footprints got on your bedroom ceiling, Lucy. When are you going to learn that you are not in a circus? Oh! I wish we'd never left you out in that storm.'

Lucy and Nicholas fell in a heap on the settee.

'Now, come and have tea. Wash your hands first.'

While they washed their hands, Nicholas and Lucy argued about how much they hated liver.

'I bet I hate it more than you do,' said Nicholas.

'You don't. I hate it so much I'd rather die than eat it.'

'Well, I hate it so much I'd rather die twice.'

'Don't be stupid!' snapped Lucy. 'How can you die twice?'

They both snatched at the towel to dry their hands. 'If you get shot with two bullets you die twice,' Nicholas claimed.

'Oh, you are so stupid sometimes. You . . .'

'Teatime!' called Mrs King. 'Haven't you two finished yet?'

When they sat down at table Mum was still busy frying the liver. Lucy wrinkled up her nose in disgust. It was one smell she couldn't stand. She glared at the frying pan and wished it would vanish in flames.

'Don't pull faces,' warned Mum. Lucy

scowled and glared even harder at the frying pan. The centres of her eyes took on a strange, flickering glow.

Suddenly there was a tremendous bang. The oven door flew off and black smoke billowed from the frying pan. Flames scuttled across the top of the cooker. Mrs King leaped backwards with a strangled cry, dropping the pan and spilling liver across the floor.

Nicholas started yelling, while Lucy simply stared with horror at the flaming gas cooker, her face as white as a ghost.

Mum seized a thick towel and flung it across the cooker. With no air to feed on, the flames quickly died. The kitchen was filled with the unpleasant stink of singed towel, but at least the flames had gone out. Mum wiped her forehead with a sooty tea towel and opened the door to let out the fumes.

Then she realized someone was crying. It was Lucy. Mrs King hurried over to her daughter.

'Lucy! Whatever is the matter? You haven't been burned, have you?'

Lucy could only shake her head and sob for a long time, but at last she huddled up against Mum and began telling her how she had wished the frying pan would go up in flames and she got this weird feeling of power and suddenly everything seemed to explode and the cooker was in flames and Nicholas was yelling and there was smoke everywhere – it was like a nightmare.

Mum's jaw dropped. 'You mean, you mean *you* made it all happen?' she asked incredulously.

Lucy nodded and burst into tears all over again. 'But I didn't mean it to. I didn't know it would happen, Mum, honestly I didn't. This strange feeling crept over me. It was horrible.'

Mrs King hugged Lucy tight. 'Don't worry. I'm sure you didn't mean to. Go and play upstairs quietly while I sort things out down here.' Lucy sniffed and went upstairs with Nicholas.

By this time the family cat, Flop, had sneaked in and run off with the burnt liver, so once Mum had cleared the kitchen she had to do a bread and butter tea. That was much more to Lucy's liking.

When Dad came in from work it took a lot of talking to explain why the cooker was black all over and the oven door only hanging on by one hinge. Lucy still looked pale and worried after her new burst of power, and she went up to bed early, leaving Mr and Mrs King to talk things over.

'She worries me,' said Mrs King. 'Is there no end to her powers? Whatever will she do next?'

'I don't like to think,' Mr King answered. 'What concerns me is how we are going to pay for a new cooker. The car practically fell to bits on the way home tonight, so that's going to need paying for. I've no idea where the money is going to come from – not when we are in the middle of all the expense of moving house as well.'

Mr King frowned for a long time. Then he looked up at his wife and smiled. 'I don't suppose Lucy might develop a power for making money?'

Mrs King laughed. 'Knowing our daughter, she would probably make it all in the wrong currency. But it does worry me, this new power. It seems to be uncontrollable.'

'Yes,' mused her husband. 'Rather like Lucy herself – uncontrollable!'

5 Whoops!

Mrs King finished reading her magazine and glanced across at her husband. He was lying on the settee with his eyes closed.

'Are you asleep?' she murmured.

He carefully opened one eye. 'Yes,' he said, 'and I'm dreaming about winning thousands of pounds so that we can buy a new cooker and car.' He sat up and looked searchingly at his wife.

'There's something on your mind,' Mr King said, 'I can tell.'

'It's Lucy. She worries me. I've got used to her being able to fly and make things move about without touching them. But this new power – making things explode into flames – it's so destructive.'

'I know,' sighed Mr King. 'I've seen the cooker — or what's left of it.'

'Lucy's other powers don't do much harm,' Mrs King went on, 'but starting fires is terribly dangerous. Suppose she has a nightmare and uses her new power in her sleep? Her whole bed might go up in flames!'

Mr King got up and put an arm round his wife. 'I'm sure she'll be all right. Let's see how things go. She's never dreamed about flying, has she? I know she's scatterbrained at times but she's a sensible girl underneath. Besides, she'll be nine shortly.'

'That's another thing,' said Mrs King. 'What are we going to do for her birthday? You know she wants a bike.'

'I don't think we can afford a bike, a new cooker and get the car repaired. Which is most useful?'

'You can't cook on a bicycle,' said Mrs King sharply.

Mr King laughed. 'You can't ride a cooker,' he pointed out. 'I take your point. Moving house is going to be another expense. The bike will have to wait. I know someone at work who's selling a cassette player second-hand. Let's get that.'

Mrs King nodded. 'OK. We'll have a little party, too.'

Although Mrs King was worried about Lucy's newly discovered power, she wasn't nearly as anxious as Lucy was herself. For days Lucy wandered about hardly daring to look at anything, in case it suddenly burst into flames. She kept her eyes almost shut, and often bumped into things as a result.

More than anything she wanted to find out how her dangerous new power worked. Then maybe she would be able to control it. But finding a chance to try it out wasn't easy.

One afternoon, when nobody was around, she went into the garden and tried staring very hard at things. She didn't have any success, and was just about to go indoors when two of Dad's best cabbages burst into flames, leaving twisted and charred stalks behind.

Lucy hurriedly buried them and hoped Dad would never find out. But she still had no idea why the cabbages had gone up in smoke and nothing else had. It was all very unsettling.

Lucy's birthday came, and luckily it was a Sunday so she didn't have to spend the day at

school. Robert came to her party, and so did
Paula, another school friend. Robert brought
her a whoopee cushion. Lucy blew it up and
stuffed it under a cushion on Paula's chair.
When Paula sat down it made the most
revolting noise and everybody was reduced to
hysterical laughter.

Paula had brought Lucy a blank cassette tape.
'It's so that you can record anything,' Paula said.
'Your cassette player's got a microphone, hasn't
it? You can record yourself.'

For the next half hour they recorded people
sitting on the whoopee cushion. They recorded
Dad leaping into the air and yelling: 'What was
that horrible noise!' They taped Mum
mumbling: 'Oooh! I do beg your pardon. I must
have eaten something that didn't agree with me.'

When teatime came they all had stomach
ache from laughing so much. Mum brought in a
birthday cake she had made herself. The candles
were lit, everybody sang 'Happy Birthday to
Lucy!' and Lucy made the cake fly round the
room before she blew the candles out.

'It was like a space ship,' said Nicholas.

'Like a flying birthday cake,' said Paula, who
liked getting things right.

When Paula and Robert were about to leave, Robert whispered in Lucy's ear, 'Are you going to bring the whoopee cushion to school tomorrow?' Lucy began to giggle. Robert went on. 'You could put it . . . you know!' He started to laugh.

'What are you two whispering about?' asked Mrs King.

'Nothing!' cried Lucy, very guiltily. 'See you tomorrow, Robert. Bye, Paula.'

'Don't forget!' shouted Robert.

Lucy stood on the steps and waved. Then she went in, collected her presents together and took them upstairs. She was looking forward to tomorrow.

As soon as Lucy got to school she got out the whoopee cushion and began showing it all round. It caused a great deal of amusement. The only person who didn't find it funny was Maureen Best. Maureen was one of those girls who was brilliant at everything, and that included telling tales. Now Maureen sauntered over and took a cool look at what was going on.

'I think that's silly,' she said. 'It's disgusting.'

'Do you want to sit on it?' offered Lucy.

'Urgh!' winced Maureen, wrinkling up her nose. 'I'd rather sit on a hippo.'

'Poor hippo,' murmured Robert.

When school started Lucy ran into class. Mr Barber hadn't got there yet so she quickly blew up the cushion and shoved it under the cover on his chair. Then she got out her reading book and sat at her desk like an angel. The class settled down.

Mr Barber came in and hung up his jacket. He sorted out some papers on his desk. Lucy held her breath. Mr Barber went to the window and opened it a fraction. He went back to his desk. Then he went to the cupboard, then back to his desk. He stood there a few moments, pulled out his chair and – sat down. PHLLURRRRRPH!!

Mr Barber just sat there until the cushion finished. The class rolled about laughing as if they'd never laughed before. When they stopped Mr Barber slowly got to his feet and pulled the whoopee cushion out. He held it up.

'I wonder whose this can be?' he asked. There was silence. Then Maureen Best stood up. Mr Barber had never been so surprised.

'Maureen! Is it yours?'

Maureen almost choked and went bright red. 'No, Mr Barber! But I know whose it is. It's Lucy King's.'

Mr Barber sighed. He didn't like people telling tales. All the same, he would have to do something, or the cushion would be turning up in class all day. He looked across at Lucy.

'Is it yours?'

Lucy nodded and waited for the anger to fall on her head, but Mr Barber smiled. 'It's very good,' he said. 'I think it's the best whoopee cushion I've sat on, but I think we'll put it somewhere safe for the time being. All right?'

Again Lucy nodded and Mr Barber put the cushion away in the cupboard. Lucy heard Maureen sniggering not far to one side of her. She glanced across and saw Maureen put her thumb to her nose, screw up her eyes and waggle her fingers.

Lucy stared back angrily. They'd all been having such good fun with the whoopee cushion. She'd been planning to take it out at playtime. Now Maureen Best was grinning madly because she'd spoilt Lucy's fun and had the whoopee cushion taken away.

Lucy rested her head on one hand and glared

across at Maureen. In turn, Maureen poked out her tongue. Lucy's eyes narrowed. A peculiar feeling crept over her, making the hair on the back of her neck prickle. Lucy's eyes began to glow red.

A wisp of smoke trailed out from the lid of Maureen's desk. Maureen sniffed several times and then looked down. The smoke was getting thicker by the second. She gave a squeak of alarm and opened her desk lid. Tongues of flame licked up from her burning books, and a moment later the sides of the desk were alight and smoke was swirling up to the ceiling.

Maureen screamed and toppled backwards off her chair in a dead faint. Mr Barber was already on his feet and yelling, 'Fire! Fire!'

Lucy sat frozen, chilled to the heart by what she had done. The sound of the fire alarm brought her back to life. The room was filling with smoke and Mr Barber was ushering the children to safety. He had Maureen Best slung over one shoulder.

Lucy knew she must act quickly. In a shower of sparks she zoomed into the air and smashed through one of the classroom windows. Like a comet she sped over the school and was soon dragging the hose out of the caretaker's shed.

The playground was full of excited children and teachers, escaping from the spreading flames. They watched in awe as Lucy connected the hose, grabbed the nozzle and went whizzing back to the classroom, with the hose snaking out behind.

There was so much smoke Lucy couldn't see through the broken window. It swirled round her making her choke violently. She pointed the nozzle into the classroom and drenched everything. The burning desk hissed and spluttered and the stench of hot water and ash billowed out, but Lucy stayed there, spraying the classroom until she was quite certain the fire had gone out. She turned off the nozzle and glanced into the dripping, blackened classroom. Lucy had never felt so miserable. Tears began to roll down her cheeks.

Mr Barber came running to her and picked her up. 'Lucy! Thank goodness you're safe. You were incredible! You've saved the school!'

This was too much for Lucy and her shoulders heaved. 'But, but, Mr Barber, it was . . . my . . . I . . . I . . .' she stammered, not knowing how to start.

Mrs Conway, the head teacher, came up, looking very concerned.

'Are you all right, Lucy?' she asked. 'It was marvellous what you did!' Then she turned to Mr Barber. 'Poor girl. I think she's a bit shocked. She must lie down and then go home. She's been a very, very brave girl.'

So Lucy went home, pale and subdued. When Mum and Dad heard the story they realized at once how the fire had started. They didn't say anything then because Lucy was so obviously upset. Besides, what could they say?

Lucy didn't know what to do next. Her new power was so uncontrollable and, much as she disliked Maureen Best, Lucy didn't want to make anybody go up in smoke, and that was what she was afraid would happen next, unless she learned how to control herself.

6 A Testing Time

For several days after the fire at school Lucy was quiet and moody. Both Mum and Dad tried to cheer her up, but with no success.

'I think she's scared,' said Mr King. 'I think she's discovered she has this extraordinary power and it frightens her. We ought to do something to try and help her.'

Mrs King laughed nervously. 'Perhaps we could strap a fire extinguisher to her back?' she suggested.

'Not a bad idea,' laughed Mr King. 'Or maybe we should give her a water pistol to carry round. No – I was wondering about taking her to see Dr Evans, or to the hospital and get some tests done.'

'What's the point? There's nothing wrong with her, Harold. The only problem is that she can fly, levitate anything she likes and make things burst into flames. That's normal – for Lucy.'

There didn't seem to be anything they could do. Then, one afternoon, Mr King was reading the newspaper when he came across an article that interested him. He mentioned it to his wife.

'There's a piece here about a Research Centre that's investigating parapsychology – you know, the strange things that some people are able to do, like bending spoons by stroking them or making things happen just by thinking about them.'

'Do they investigate people who can fly through the air?' asked Mrs King, half jokingly.

'That's just it. Why shouldn't they be able to help with Lucy? Perhaps they can find out how she makes things explode?'

'I suppose it's worth a try if it will help Lucy,' Mrs King said slowly. 'Give them a ring in the morning.'

The Research Centre was very interested when they heard about Lightning Lucy, and they asked Mr King to bring her along as soon as possible. Mr King took a day off work and drove Lucy to the Centre, an old rambling house set in huge grounds.

'I wouldn't mind living here,' Dad said to Lucy as they drove up the drive.

'It's too big,' said Lucy. 'And I bet it's got ghosts.'

'You're not scared of ghosts, are you?'

'No, of course not!' lied Lucy. 'But I expect Nicholas is.'

They were greeted at the Centre by a large, breathless man wearing thick spectacles that made his eyes seem twice as large as normal. 'Hallo, hallo!' he boomed. 'I'm Professor Brownsmith-Jones and you must be Lucy. Hallo, Lucy! I'm Professor Brownsmith – bother, I've told you that already, haven't I? No point in telling you again, is there? Well, come in, come in, come in. Don't stand on the doorstep like . . . um, like people . . . er . . . standing on the doorstep. Ha ha! Silly me!' The professor showed them into his study, still chuckling away to himself. He sat them down on chairs and seated himself behind his desk in a huge leather swivel chair.

'Well!' he cried. 'I hear you can do all sorts of

special things, Lucy. Perhaps you'd show me, eh?'

Lucy looked blankly at Dad. 'What shall I do?' she whispered. Mr King smiled encouragingly.

'Why don't you fly round the room a little?'

It seemed a strange thing to ask and Lucy felt rather silly flying slowly round the room with nothing to do. Whenever she had flown before it was for a special purpose. She slipped back to her chair and sat down, whilst the faint red glow slowly faded from her body.

Professor Brownsmith-Jones had risen from his chair and he stood in the middle of the room with his eyes almost popping out from the sides of his spectacles.

'Did I see what I think I saw?' he demanded.

'Yes,' said Mr King rather proudly.

The professor began to walk quickly in tight circles, round and round, talking all the time. 'This is quite, quite extraordinary. Quite amazing! A girl who can fly, and why can a girl fly? I don't know. Does anybody know? I should think not, and why don't they know? Because they've never asked. What haven't they asked? I don't know, because I've forgotten what I'm talking about and I'm feeling rather dizzy so I'd better sit down. Where is everything?'

He stood still and waited for the room to stop swimming round him. Then he stared across at Lucy. 'And what else can you do?' he demanded.

'I can make things float,' said Lucy.

'Make things float?' The professor looked a trifle disappointed. 'Like boats?'

'No. Float in the air.'

'Oh! You mean like planes?' suggested the professor.

'You'd better show him,' murmured Dad. So Lucy got up and pointed at the professor and before he could say 'help!' he found himself rising into the air.

'Help!' he squeaked, when he overcame his own surprise. 'Put me down, please, I can't stand heights!'

Lucy gently allowed the professor to land on the carpet. He got out a large handkerchief and mopped his sweating brow.

'I mean float like that,' explained Lucy.

'It's quite amazing,' gabbled the professor. 'Most unusual. I must do some tests at once and find out where your power is coming from.' He squinted at Lucy suspiciously.

'You haven't got special batteries hidden in your socks, have you?'

Lucy spluttered at the very idea, and shook her head. Mr King grinned quietly to himself, and the professor sighed.

'Well, you must come through into the laboratory and I'll connect you up to my new multi-positronic electro-defeebilizer.'

Lucy looked anxiously back at her father. He smiled and winked at her. 'You'll be all right,' he said. 'I won't be far away.' Lucy bit her lip and trailed after the professor.

The laboratory was enormous. It ticked and clicked and hummed with a hundred different gadgets. Rows of TV monitors along one wall displayed heartbeats, pulse rates and brainwaves. In one corner a large computer chattered away to itself.

But what Lucy noticed most of all was the massive chair in the centre of the room. It was like a dentist's chair, only wider and longer. Wires sprouted from all over it and trailed away to mysterious boxes. Little lights flashed on and off. The professor hurried around switching things on and tapping dials. He pointed at the chair.

'You hop up there and I'll get you connected up. Now why won't the anti-static googlebender come on? You're a silly thing, aren't you? Yes, you are!'

While the professor talked to his instruments, Lucy climbed on to the chair and lay back. She gazed up at the ceiling and saw, for the first time, a weird machine hanging there. It glittered with reflected light, and looked like nothing so much as an alien spaceship. Lucy shivered.

'Ah! Good girl,' cried the professor. 'Now, I'll pop the electro-defeebilizer on.' He flicked a switch and the machine slowly descended, humming quietly to itself. It hovered above Lucy's curls. She squeezed herself down into the chair, away from the glistening metal gadget.

'No need to worry,' said the professor cheerfully. 'It's quite harmless. See, I'm wearing it myself.' He fitted the headpiece over his own bald dome, gave a little jump and a squeak, and whipped the headpiece off quickly. 'Ooh! Just a tiny shock! Nothing to worry about!'

Lucy smiled to herself. Electric shocks were one thing that she *was* used to. After all, she'd had lightning go right through her. The professor dropped the headpiece over her and she felt a warm tingle. Lucy settled back and relaxed.

Professor Brownsmith-Jones fastened something round her wrists. 'These bands will record your pulse,' he explained. He fastened a wider band across her stomach. 'This one will tell me what you had for breakfast. Ha ha ha! Silly me, just a joke. Comfortable? Yes, yes. Don't run away now, and off we go.'

He danced from one instrument to the next, flicking switches. The room vibrated with the steady hum of electricity, and dials began to twitter away. Little lights blinked on and off. Spurts of paper came from the computer.

'Fantastic, fantastic!' cried the professor, looking from one thing to the next. 'It's all working. My goodness, yes. I can see from your pulse rate you're still alive. That's a good thing. Let's see what happens when we switch on the multi-positronic electro-defeebilizer!'

He plugged a fistful of coloured wires into Lucy's headpiece and immediately Lucy felt very weird. It was the strangest feeling she had ever experienced, as if all the inside parts of her body were rushing upwards, leaving her skin to struggle after it, longing to catch up.

Her head swam, and it seemed that her brain was filled with tiny dots of light, flashing on and off. It was altogether horrible and made her feel ill. Lucy wanted to stop. She tried to open her mouth to call out, but her lips wouldn't move and her tongue felt huge and useless. Her whole body felt huge and useless and the lights inside her head flashed ever brighter and faster, like warning signals spelling out danger.

Lucy screwed up her eyes and desperately tried to concentrate her thoughts on the defeebilizer, certain that it was the cause of her nightmare. Her brain was filled with a whirring noise that steadily grew louder. The chair started to tremble and its castors jiggled on the floor. A red haze surrounded the whole unit and tiny sparks began to dart from Lucy's fingers and hair.

A deep, low hum rumbled throughout the lab and Lucy's chair lifted from the ground and rose towards the ceiling, slowly swinging round as it did so. Brownsmith-Jones gave a startled cry and leaped towards it.

'Come back! Come down!' he yelled, and grabbed hold of the passing foot rest. It didn't do him any good. The professor left the ground

for the second time that morning. He clung
frantically to the bottom of the chair and closed
his eyes.

The whole laboratory was now filled with the
rising drone of over-charged electricity. Machines
began to rattle and bounce on their shelves and
Lucy crackled all over and thin whiplashes of
sparks leaped from her body.

The TV monitors began to rise into the air.
Everything in the lab began to take off, lifting up
to the ceiling and trailing wires behind like a
hundred kite strings. The smaller instruments
flew up from their shelves and whizzed across
the room from side to side. Tweezers clattered
against the window. Scissors clanged against
cupboards and some of the sharper tools flung
themselves at the walls and ceiling and stuck
there, quivering.

Meanwhile the computer was churning out
paper messages faster and faster and the entire
floor was now covered with a thick carpet of
computer printout. Stuck up high against the
ceiling, Professor Brownsmith-Jones screamed for
assistance. 'Help!!'

Mr King burst into the lab, crunching across a
sea of paper. He twisted and ducked as

instruments whistled past his head, threatening to slice his ears and nose off.

'Switch everything off!' pleaded the professor from on high.

Mr King raced round the room flicking and unplugging. The hum subsided. The machines slowly descended and piled themselves up on the shelves and floor. The great chair landed safely and Professor Brownsmith-Jones slumped to the floor, groaning. Lucy's eyelids flickered. Dad bent over her anxiously.

'Are you all right?' he asked. Lucy opened her eyes and smiled up at him. She gave a long sigh.

'It started off horrid,' she said. 'But then it got better and better. I had a lovely dream. I dreamt the whole world was taking off.'

'You weren't far wrong,' said Dad. Then Lucy saw all the paper and mess and the professor still groaning on the floor.

'Is Mr Brownblackgreen all right?' she asked.

'Brownsmith-Jones,' mumbled the professor. 'Brownsmith-Jones, Brownsmith-Jones. I think I'm dead. Can you take my pulse for me? I'm sure I'm dead and this must be hell. Oh dear, oh dear.'

Mr King and Lucy helped the professor to get

up and tidy the lab. The poor professor had to admit that there was nothing he could do to help. His instruments had been unable to record Lucy's powers at all. She was simply too strong for them.

'I could hardly believe it,' the professor exclaimed as he said goodbye to them. 'Everything just went out of control.'

'Yes,' said Mr King, shaking the professor's hand. 'Lucy does have that effect on things rather.' Hearing this, Lucy went quiet. She began to wish that just for once she could do something helpful.

7 Lucy Gives the Piano a Lesson

Lucy and Nicholas were not looking forward to moving for two reasons. First of all they hated the idea of leaving the old house. It was like being told to throw out a favourite jumper. The second reason was that their moving day fell on the same day as the Grand Summer Fair, which took place in the park. They would miss everything.

Mr King tried to cheer them up. 'You'll soon get used to the new house, and we might get some peace and quiet there too, if Lucy doesn't do anything too spectacular for a while.' He wrapped some plates and packed them into a big wooden crate.

Lucy and Nicholas were soon involved in

packing their own bedrooms. Everything had to go into boxes, and by the time moving day came, almost the whole house had been shoved into packing cases and stacked downstairs, ready to go. Only the beds had to be dismantled and the carpets rolled up.

'Do remember that the removal men are going to be working very hard,' said Mrs King. 'Don't get in their way.'

'Can't we help at all?' asked Lucy.

'Yes, you can help at the other end by unpacking your boxes and putting your clothes away neatly.'

'Oh, that will be great fun!' groaned Lucy. 'Won't that be exciting, Nicky?'

Mrs King turned on her daughter. 'Don't call him Nicky!'

'But really, I prefer being called Nicky,' admitted Nicholas.

'Oh for goodness' sake! Don't you start too. As if we haven't got enough to think about today. Now please keep out of the way.'

'But I could be really useful,' Lucy protested. 'I could make things float into the new house, and the removal men wouldn't have to do anything at all.'

But Mrs King went on shaking her head. 'Definitely not. I don't think I could cope with flying wardrobes and supersonic armchairs today. Please keep out of it.'

Mr King came in and told Lucy and Nicholas to go and play for a while, while they got the van loaded. Reluctantly, the two children went off, with much grumbling and groaning.

It took ages to load the van. Lucy and Nicholas watched from an upstairs window as the removal men went backwards and forwards carrying load after load. Into the van went cupboards and chairs and boxes and carpets and the TV and the fridge and the new cooker – everything. There was only one thing left.

Lucy hoped they would leave the piano behind, but no, there it went, rumbling down the path like some strange, stiff dinosaur. The van had an air-operated tail gate, so once the piano was on the gate it was hoisted to the same height as the van. All the men had to do was push it inside.

Lucy wrinkled up her nose in disgust and went downstairs. The house looked odd now that it was empty. It didn't feel like their house at all.

'We're ready to go,' called Mum. They piled

into the car and set off in front of the van. Half way there the car broke down.

'What a wonderful start,' shouted Dad, kicking a front tyre angrily. The removal van had to tow them the rest of the way.

The new house was almost at the top of a steep hill. At the bottom was the town centre, and at the top a rambling park where the Grand Summer Fair was always held. When the van pulled up outside the new house, the road was already full of excited people. Some were hurrying down to see the big band parade and watch all the floats go by. Others were struggling up the hill, to get to the park and join in the fun. Nobody wanted to miss anything.

'Just our luck,' groaned Lucy. 'We'll miss everything.'

But Mr King had other ideas. He put one hand in his trouser pocket. 'Lucy, Nicholas! I think the best thing for you to do is go off and enjoy the fair while Mum and I sort things out. I'll give you five pounds, all right? Don't spend it all at once.'

Dad fished a five-pound note from his pocket and handed it over. Nicholas danced round and round shouting with delight, but Lucy carefully held the money up to the light and peered hard at it.

'Is it real?' she asked. 'Is it a genuine five-pound note?'

Dad gave her a playful punch. 'Cheeky devil! Go and enjoy yourselves. But don't get into any trouble!' He watched them set off down the hill. Mrs King came over and slipped one arm through his. 'That was a good idea,' she said. 'Now perhaps we shall be able to unpack in peace.'

It didn't take long for Lucy and Nicholas to quarrel over what they would do first. Nicholas wanted to go straight to the park and Lucy wanted to see the floats. But when Lucy told Nicholas there'd be a Formula I racing car in the procession, he agreed to go down to the High Street.

'How do you know it's going to be there?' asked Nicholas.

'Robert told me. He knows Gary Burnett and Gary's dad owns the big garage near the school. I think the racing car has something to do with him because I saw a photo, and there's "Burnett's Garage" written all down both sides.'

Nicholas frowned. 'What? Why does Mr Burnett want writing down his sides?'

'Not Mr Burnett's sides, you dope,' groaned Lucy. 'Down the sides of the racing car. It's for advertising.'

When they reached the bottom of the hill the parade had already started. Round the corner it came, with the band in the lead and the floats behind. The brass instruments shone in the sun. The trumpets blared and the drums boomed. Everybody shouted and cheered and waved. Lucy and Nicholas soon got caught up with watching everything, and quite forgot that they were in the middle of moving house.

Near the top of the hill the house moving was going quite well, with Nicholas and Lucy safely out of the way. The last thing to be moved was the piano. The removal men got it down from the van all right, but they had great difficulty getting it up the kerb, which was very high. There were only two men and the piano was extremely heavy.

'Hang on,' said one. 'I'll come to your end and give a hand.' Then as soon as he let go of his end the piano began to roll sideways down the hill.

'Grab it quick!' yelled the second man, and he threw himself after the piano, but his weight only helped shove the piano faster on its way. The great instrument slipped from his grasp and trundled away down the hill, rapidly gaining speed.

Cars coming up the hill suddenly found themselves trying to dodge a rumbling, roaring monster charging down the hill in great zigzags. The cars screeched and swerved, hooters honking, and there were several near misses as the piano raced past.

A crowd of people came chasing pell-mell after the runaway, shouting advice above the thundering echoes of the piano strings and the zinging of the little metal castors on the road.

'Stop that piano!'

'Call the police!'

'Watch out!'

Nobody at the bottom of the hill could hear them because of the parade. The band went trumpeting round the corner and up the hill, and down the hill came the speeding piano, intent upon joining them. The band went wild, scattering in all directions as the piano cut a path straight through their midst. Trumpets and drums were left in the middle of the road. The music became a series of shrill squeaks, and the crowd joined in with their shouts of panic.

With all that noise going on it was little wonder that Lucy thought something had gone wrong. She ran to the corner and looked around. There was chaos everywhere, with frightened bandsmen shinning up lamp posts and women snatching their children to safety as the piano thundered past them down the hill.

Without thinking twice Lucy was up in the air and swooping low across the panicking crowds, leaving a long trail of glorious sparks behind. She zoomed up behind the piano and pointed her outstretched arms at it. A stream of glittering red came from her fingertips, gathering round the rattling monster. Lucy concentrated her mind, intent upon slowing the death trap down. From the corner of her eye Lucy became aware of people and shops and cars, all rushing into view.

In a moment she knew that she couldn't slow the piano down in time. It was certain to crash, with terrifying results. She summoned up all her power and glared furiously at the instrument.

The lid flew off. The sides blew apart. Smoke poured from the top and in a flash of gold it burst into flames and collapsed on the spot, just a few metres from the racing car, whose driver had leaped out and was trying to hide under a giant tuba.

Somebody ran forward with a fire extinguisher and sprayed the smoking remains of the piano. Lucy landed on the pavement and wiped her brow. It had been a close thing. Instantly she was surrounded by people, yet she felt strangely awkward. It was bound to lead to more attention and that was just what Mum and Dad didn't want. As soon as she could she gave everybody the slip, found Nicholas and went quietly home.

Mr and Mrs King were sitting in the front room, surrounded by unpacked boxes, listening to Nicholas telling them all that had happened.

'Why does it always happen to you?' asked Mrs King, when he'd finished. Lucy was silent. 'That was our best piano too. Now you've got nothing to practise on.'

They were interrupted by a knock at the door. Standing outside was Mr Burnett. 'I've just popped up from the garage to say thank you. That was incredible, Lucy! I could hardly believe my eyes. I was sure that piano was going to smash my racing car to pulp. I could see hundreds of thousands of pounds vanishing in front of my eyes. Then you swooped down and wham! Amazing! I'm very grateful.'

Mr Burnett sat down and talked for a while. Lucy went upstairs. She wanted to be by herself. She lay on her bed and stared gloomily at the ceiling. She heard the front door bang.

'Lucy!' Dad was calling from the bottom of the stairs. 'Lucy, come down!' Mum and Dad and Nicholas were waiting in the front room. They were all grinning like monkeys.

'I don't know how you do it,' said Mr King. 'Mr Burnett was so pleased by the way you saved his racing car that he's going to get rid of our old car for us and give us a new one to replace it. Well, almost new anyway. How about that?'

Lucy gasped. 'What? A new car? Really? Really and truly?'

'Really and truly,' laughed Mum.

'Yippee!' cried Lucy. Perhaps life wasn't so bad after all. They were getting a new car and she wouldn't have to do piano practice any more because she'd just blown the piano up.

'And I had another brainwave,' said Dad, smiling. 'Our old piano was insured. All we have to do is put in a claim and we can get a new piano for Lucy to practise on. After all, it's only fair. If she can get me a new car, the least I can do is get her a new piano.'

'Aren't you lucky,' teased Mum.

Lucy let out a long groan and pretended to faint.

Lightning Lucy
Storms Ahead

1 The Witch's Cat

Lucy King sat at her desk in class and stared at the page of maths in front of her. She stared so hard that the numbers started to wiggle and change. She shut her eyes tight.

'Don't go to sleep, Lucy,' said Mr Barber from the front of the class. 'You've only been in school half an hour. Bedtime isn't for another ten hours.'

Lucy glanced up at her teacher, red with embarrassment. She nudged Paula beside her. 'How do you do number four?'

'It's easy,' her friend hissed back, which wasn't much help.

'It's only easy if you know how to do it,' Lucy pointed out. 'If you don't know, then it's very difficult. So how do you do it?'

Paula put down her pencil. 'If I show you how to do this, promise you'll give me a ride after school?'

Lucy nodded.

'Right then,' said Paula. 'This number is bigger than that so it goes there. Take that away from that because you don't need it. That leaves you with 573, now add on from over there and divide the remainder and add it on to your first bit and there you are – *that's* the answer. See, it's easy.'

'I feel giddy,' murmured Lucy, as Paula pushed her book back.

'Don't forget that ride after school,' Paula went on. 'Then you can come and see our kittens if you want.'

'Kittens! Has your cat had kittens?'

'She's had five. There's a tiny tabby one and two black and ginger ones, only one has got this silly white tip on his . . .'

'Paula Lewis and Lucy King! Stop gabbling and get on with your maths,' shouted Mr Barber.

The two girls bent over their work. They had to wait until playtime before Paula could finish her catalogue of kittens. Then they had to wait until after school before they had a chance to actually see them. Lucy asked if her young brother, Nicholas, could come too.

'Don't forget you said I could have a ride,' Paula said. 'As soon as we get to my garden.'

'Why are you giving her a ride?' Nicholas asked. 'Mum said you mustn't give anybody rides. She doesn't like you showing off.'

'Never you mind,' said Lucy. 'Just be quiet.'

'But why are you giving her a ride? You don't give me rides.'

'I do – lots of times. Just be quiet, will you? Paula helped me with some maths and I said I'd give her a ride in return.'

Nicholas walked on, thinking hard. 'All right, then give me a ride too and I'll help you with your maths.'

Lucy just laughed and called him an idiot. Nicholas pulled a dark scowl and stamped on ahead. Sometimes his sister could be a real pain, even if she did have amazing powers.

The trouble was that Lucy King was rather special. Strange things had happened to her. When she was only a few months old her pram had been struck by lightning. Instead of being harmed, baby Lucy seemed to enjoy it. Her whole pram glowed and crackled with electricity.

Her parents thought it was a miracle that she had escaped and eventually forgot all about it, until a few years later, when Lucy fell into a garden pond. Before her parents could rush to save her, Lucy zoomed out of the pond and up into a tree. She could fly! Over the next few years they discovered that not only could Lucy fly, but she could make objects float around. Just lately she had developed a rather weird power of making things burst into flames.

Of course, Lucy started using her powers. She stopped a runaway coach from crashing. She rounded up an entire herd of rampaging cattle in the High Street. People began to notice her zooming about, and soon she got the nickname, Lightning Lucy, because she glowed and crackled with electric power. Sometimes you could see little sparks darting from her charged-up body.

However, being famous and special had its drawbacks and Lucy's parents did not want her to get big-headed or use her powers without good cause. They certainly did not like her giving people rides by making them float round the garden, and that was exactly what Lucy was now doing with Paula. She was standing in the centre of the garden, pointing both hands at her friend. Lucy's tumbledown hair was sticking out all over, with tiny sparks dancing in it as Paula floated idly round the garden on her back, grinning madly.

Paula rolled on to her tummy and began to make swimming movements. 'Look! I can swim in the air!' she shouted. Nicholas watched jealously as Lucy lowered her hands and brought Paula in to land. 'That was great! Fantastic!'

'I want to see the kittens,' complained Nicholas.

'Yes, come on, where are the kittens?' Lucy demanded, shaking the crackles out of her curls.

Paula took them into the kitchen. There was a table pushed into one corner and underneath, at the very back, was a big cardboard box with the front cut away. Curled inside was the mother cat with her five kittens, struggling all over her like half-blind mountaineers. Paula gently picked out two kittens and handed them over.

'They're beautiful,' Nicholas murmured.

'You can have one if you want,' said Paula. 'We're looking for homes for all of them.'

'We could have two!' suggested Lucy. 'We'll ask Mum and Dad. I like that black and ginger one with the white tail.'

'I like this tabby,' crooned Nicholas, holding it up and staring into its face. 'He's got a moustache. Look.'

Reluctantly they put the kittens back because the mother was beginning to look worried. The children backed out from beneath the table and soon Lucy and Nicholas were racing home with the news.

'Paula's had kittens!' shouted Lucy. Mrs King's eyes opened wide.

'How extraordinary! Paula's had kittens? Does her mother know? I should think she'll be most surprised.'

Lucy giggled and pulled her mother's arm. 'Oh, you know, Mum! Her cat's had kittens and they're all beautiful and . . .'

'. . . Paula said you could have one. The answer is no,' said her mother.

Nicholas grinned. 'Paula said we could have two.'

'The answer is still no. What about poor Flop?'

'Oh please, Mum. They're absolutely angelic.'

Mrs King shook her head. 'I can remember when Flop was a kitten and looked angelic. Look at him now – he's more like a stuffed fur coat.'

Lucy and Nicholas went on and on but their mother would not give way. As soon as Mr King came in from work they started again, describing each kitten in turn.

'They sound beautiful,' said their father.

'They ARE beautiful!' Lucy shouted.

'I like kittens,' said Mr King.

'So do we!' Nicholas yelled.

Mrs King looked across at her husband. She could see which way the conversation was going. 'What about Flop? Suppose he doesn't like it?'

'Let's ask him,' said Mr King, and he got down on his stomach in front of their old cat, who was half asleep on the floor. 'Well, Flop, would you like a kitten for a friend?'

Flop turned his head away, yawned, shut his eyes and went to sleep. Mr King looked up at his wife and grinned.

Mrs King groaned. 'Oh, go on then. But only one kitten, mind you,' she shouted as Lucy and Nicholas dashed to the telephone to ring Paula.

Five weeks later a new kitten came to the house. It was the tabby that Nicholas had fancied, and the whole family agreed that with a white moustache like that he would have to be called Colonel.

Colonel quickly became used to his new home and he would dash madly around, sinking teeth into one thing and claws into another. For some strange, kittenish reason, Colonel decided one day that Flop would make a good plaything. He raced up to the old cat and threw himself on to Flop's back. Flop had been fast asleep. He woke with a startled miaow, turned on the kitten and, spitting furiously, chased Colonel into the garden and straight up the big tree. There Colonel stayed, mewing sadly in the topmost branches until Mrs King noticed. She called her husband.

'He's stuck,' she pointed out. 'Now what do we do?'

'Maybe Lucy can fly up there,' suggested Mr King. But Lucy said she couldn't get in amongst all those thin branches.

'I could levitate him down. I'll just lift him out of the tree by thinking about it and float him back to earth.'

She raised her hands and pointed her fingers at Colonel. A startled expression came over his face as he felt an invisible force plucking at his tiny body. He dug his claws deep into the bark, clutching on for dear life.

'Silly thing,' said Lucy. 'He doesn't know I'm trying to help. It's no good. He won't move.'

'I could climb up there,' said Nicholas.

'What? That high?' asked Mr King. 'Are you sure it's safe?'

'Of course. I've done it lots of times.' Nicholas was already amongst the first branches. For once he felt brave and useful. It was pretty hard having an amazing sister like Lucy, so it was comforting to have a moment of glory.

'I'm coming,' he called up to the kitten. 'You stay there and we'll have you down in a jiffy.'

Higher and higher he went, with Lucy shouting encouragement and Mr and Mrs King growing more and more nervous about him falling.

'I'm all right,' Nicholas called down.

The cat was so scared by now that, as Nicholas came nearer, he scrambled even higher into the thinnest branches. The whole treetop was waving and wobbling as Nicholas struggled to reach the kitten.

'Take care,' warned Mr King.

'I'm OK.'

Nicholas leaned out towards Colonel. Suddenly there was a sharp crack and the branch broke.

'Help!' screamed Nicholas as he plunged earthwards, with the branch and the kitten.

Lucy had already lifted her arms, and was calmly pointing at the tumbling branch. Power surged out through her fingers and her hair glittered with sparks. The branch slowed until it was floating down gently, with Nicholas sitting astride it like a witch, an enormous grin on his face. Colonel sat up front, still clutching the bark and wondering what was going on, while the branch went round and round the garden. Nicholas had a ride after all.

'Whheeeeee!' he yelled. 'This is ace!'

Mr and Mrs King breathed sighs of relief as the witch and his cat came into land. As soon as his four paws touched solid ground, Colonel disappeared like a flash, back into the house. Lucy shook out her curls and laughed.

'I knew that kitten would mean trouble,' said Mrs King.

Nicholas and Lucy just looked at each other. Trouble? That hadn't been trouble. It had been brilliant!

2 Spot the Difference

The door of the front room was shut tight, but it did not stop strange sounds coming out. There was a low twang and throb of noise. Lucy was doing her piano practice. She had taken the front panel off the piano and was busily bashing all the wires inside. It was a wonderful noise. She listened to the bongings and clongings vibrate and die away before she set up a new clatter of pings and plonks.

The door was thrown open and Mrs King glared at her daughter. 'Is that what you call piano practice? You're meant to be playing in the Music Festival soon! I've never heard such a racket. Put that panel back at once and do your practice.' The door slammed.

Lucy gulped and quietly replaced the front of the piano. She sat on the stool and looked at her music. It was called *Ten Tin Soldiers* and it went plonk, plonk, plonk all the way through. Lucy found it almost as exciting as a wet face-flannel. That was the problem with playing the piano. When she listened to other pianists it sounded marvellous, but when she played it herself it just went plonk, plonk, plonk . . . unless she took the front panel off . . .

'Get on with your practice!' yelled her mother through the door. Lucy began to go over some scales. Mum was obviously in a Bad Mood. She had not been well recently and had even had some tests done at the hospital. Lucy didn't know what was wrong but she had noticed that her mother seemed unusually short-tempered lately.

If only there was some way she could use her powers to play the piano. She could fly through the air, make things float about the room and, if she got angry, she could even make things burst into flames – like the time she had made Maureen's desk catch fire at school – but she couldn't use her power to play the piano. Plonk, plonk, plonk. Her fingers kept getting mixed up.

It sounded as if the Ten Tin Soldiers were all marching in different directions, bumping into each other and crashing to the ground.

The door opened and Nicholas poked his head round.

'Oh, sorry. I thought there'd been an accident in here?'

'Accident?' echoed Lucy.

'I heard all the noise and thought something had fallen over.'

'Oh ha ha, very funny,' grunted Lucy, launching into another awful scale. Nicholas sat down and watched her for a few minutes.

'I wish I could play the piano,' he said eventually.

Lucy carried on playing, a touch faster and more elegantly.

'I can't play anything,' muttered Nicholas.

Lucy went on. 'Why don't you learn the piano?' she asked.

'It's too difficult.'

Lucy smiled to herself and played her scales even faster. Her fingers almost tripped over themselves, but not quite. 'It's not that difficult,' she said, 'once you know how.'

'I don't see how you can make two hands do

different things at the same time,' said Nicholas.

Lucy swelled with pride. 'It's quite easy when you know how, if you keep practising.' The scale speeded up until at last her fingers got wedged in a knot and the whole piece fell to bits. She turned on her stool. 'Just practice – that's all it needs.'

'I'm going to learn the trumpet when I'm older,' said Nicholas. 'You only need one hand to play the trumpet.'

'You need the other to hold it up,' Lucy pointed out.

Nicholas picked up the newspaper he had brought in. 'Have you seen this?' he asked, pointing at a couple of drawings in the paper.

'What is it?'

'A competition – Spot the Difference. If we spot all the changes in the picture, we could win a cross-channel ferry trip to France.'

'Go to France? Great!' shouted Lucy, snatching the paper.

Nicholas grabbed it back. 'It says here that the winner will get tickets for a car and family of four. Only it's very difficult.'

'Let me see too,' grumbled Lucy, sitting on the settee and peering over Nicholas's shoulder.

'There's one, look. That car has got an aerial missing.' Nicholas ringed the aerial. 'What about that ship? It hasn't got a porthole and the other one has.'

'That's just a spot of ink on the paper,' declared Nicholas.

'It's a missing porthole,' claimed Lucy.

'It isn't.'

'Is!'

The door opened again, Mrs King stood there glaring at them. Nicholas quietly folded the paper and went out, while Lucy crept back to the piano and started marching the Ten Tin Soldiers once more. Her mother watched her stonily and then shut the door. Slowly the Ten Tin Soldiers went off course as Lucy dreamily thought about France.

At long last Mrs King told Lucy she could stop. 'I don't think I can listen to much more,' she said. Then she saw Lucy's face and tried to smile. 'I'm sorry, Lucy. It wasn't that bad. You can do some more later. I'm just feeling off-colour today.'

Lucy slipped round her mother and went upstairs to find Nicholas and the competition.

He had already ringed seven differences. 'But I can't see any more. It's a cheat. They just say there are ten but there aren't really and then nobody wins the prize and they don't have to give away free tickets.'

'There's one,' said Lucy, ringing a missing eyebrow on a sailor's face. 'If you win this, you've got to share the prize with me.'

'Don't be daft. I've got to share it with the family anyhow.'

'I don't suppose we shall win,' murmured Lucy.

Nicholas looked at his sister. 'I don't care if *you* don't win, but *I'm* going to,' he said.

Lucy pointed out the last two mistakes and then wandered downstairs, while Nicholas wrote out his name and address and put the whole thing in an envelope.

Mrs King was resting downstairs, with her feet up on a dining chair. Lucy went and sat next to her. 'Are you all right, Mum?'

'Yes. It's just that there is so much to do and I haven't the energy to do it.'

Lucy was seized with a sudden desire to help. 'What can I do?'

Mrs King eyed her daughter, trying to think of a job that was reasonably safe. She had been helped by Lucy before, and it usually ended up with Mrs King having to do twice as much work as was necessary. 'I need some shopping: potatoes, cat food and a chicken for supper.'

'Nicholas and I can get those when he posts his letter.'

'What letter?' asked their mother and Lucy told her about the competition.

'We'd be lucky to win that,' laughed Mrs King. 'There's a spare stamp in my purse you can use. Take a ten pound note for the shopping. And Lucy!' Mrs King wagged a finger. 'Don't do anything special. *Please!*'

Lucy looked at her in amazement. 'We're only going shopping,' she pointed out.

That meant anything could happen.

They posted the letter on the way down the hill but not until they had each kissed it twice to bring it good luck and crossed their fingers. Then they stood and looked at the postbox as if they expected it to jump up and run down the High Street with their ever-so-important mail.

The supermarket was crowded.

'I wish we could fly round and pluck the things we want from the shelves,' whispered Lucy. 'How many potatoes do you think we should get?'

Nicholas said that Mum usually got lots, so

they picked up a five kilogram bag. They added several tins of cat food, but Nicholas said it wouldn't last very long, so they got a few extra.

By the time they had bought the chicken as well, Lucy could hardly carry the shopping basket.

'Why don't you carry it for a bit?' demanded Lucy, when her arm began to feel as if it was breaking right off.

Nicholas took hold of the handle and immediately dropped the whole lot on the pavement.

'I can't carry it,' he wailed. 'Only Superman could carry that!'

They stood there and eyed the ultra-heavy basket. Neither of them intended to pick it up.

'OK,' said Lucy at last. 'There's only one thing to do. I'll make it fly home. Come on, basket, up you get. Don't just lie there like that.'

Nicholas smiled as the basket hovered into the air. Up the hill they went, while the basket floated quietly above them.

At length a police car passed them, going slowly down the hill. The driver stared at the children and the floating basket. Then the car went slowly up the hill, with the driver still gawping at them. Then the car came back a third time and stopped. A young policeman got out and eyed the hovering shopping.

'Excuse me,' he began. 'But did you know that you're being followed?'

'Followed?' asked Lucy innocently. 'What by?'

'Sounds odd, miss, but you are being followed by a shopping basket.'

'Shopping?'

'Yes. Some potatoes, lots of cat food and a frozen chicken.'

'That's our shopping!' said Nicholas proudly.

'We've just bought it,' Lucy explained.

'Oh.' The policeman didn't know what to say next, so Lucy and her brother went on home, with the basket still floating above them, and the policeman slowly following in his car. The children disappeared indoors. A moment later the policeman was knocking at the door. Mrs King answered it. She guessed straight away that it was something to do with Lucy. The policeman began a long story about flying shopping baskets and children.

'You must be new around here,' said Mrs King, and she explained all about her extraordinary daughter. 'The other policemen know her well.'

'I must admit I got a bit of a shock. I wondered what I could say back at the police station. They'd think me mad if I said I'd seen a flying basket full of cat food.'

'I have told Lucy not to use her powers in that way,' said Mrs King, a bit crossly.

The young policeman smiled. 'It did look a very heavy basket,' he pointed out sympathetically. 'Your daughter must be rather special to you, with powers like that.'

There was a tremendous noise from inside which sounded as if an entire brass band had just fallen through the roof and landed in a heap on the front-room carpet. Mrs King gave a weak smile.

'Yes, I suppose she is. That noise is Lucy doing her own rather special kind of piano practice.'

The policeman stuffed his fingers in his ears and left hurriedly.

3 Slide to Disaster

'When I grow up,' said Lucy's friend Paula one day in school, 'I'm going to be a teacher. Then I shall tell people what to do all day long.'

Lucy looked at her seriously. 'I'm going to be a footballer,' she said. 'And I shall marry Robert.'

Paula gave a loud splutter that got half the class staring at her. Mr Barber, their teacher, stopped the story he was reading to them and glared silently at the girls. Paula shut her lips tight and tried to hold them in place with her teeth. Her eyes began to water.

'Robert!' she hissed. 'You can't marry Robert!'

'Why not?' Lucy demanded hotly.

'I always thought you'd marry someone like Superman.'

'Urgh,' said Lucy. 'His neck is as thick as an elephant's leg.'

Paula spluttered again and this time she got sent out of the room. Mr Barber gave Lucy a warning glance and went on with the story, but Lucy only half listened. She kept opening the crumpled message in her hand. In heavy pencil on one side was written:

To Lucy. I love you. Robert.

Lucy was wondering what to write back.

'There,' said Mr Barber, 'we'll carry on with that another day. Lucy, tell Paula to come back in now, if she's quite finished making those peculiar noises. Before you go home, here's a letter to take to your parents. It's about a fun outing for the end of the summer term,' said Mr Barber as he handed out the letters.

'Where are we going, Mr Barber?' asked Lucy.

'Ice-skating. There's a . . .'

Mr Barber's voice was drowned in an excited babble. He waited patiently until there was calm. 'As I was saying, there is a new ice rink at Gillingham and we . . .'

'I've been there,' shouted Leroy. 'It's brill!'

'Thank you, Leroy,' said Mr Barber. 'I'm sure

we shall all enjoy it. Don't forget to show your parents the letter and bring back the slip with the money. We are going next week.'

The class left school in great excitement. 'I've never been ice-skating before,' said Paula. 'Have you?'

Lucy shook her head.

'I've been lots of times,' said Maureen next to them. 'I've got my own skating boots,' she added with a smirk. She put her bag over her shoulder and walked off.

'Trust Maureen to have her own skates,' muttered Paula.

But Lucy didn't mind, as long as she and Nicholas could go on the outing. Lucy found her brother and they hurried home, anxious to discover if they would be allowed to go. Nicholas tried to practise skating on the way, but it was pretty difficult when the pavement was bone dry and he was wearing trainers.

Their father was home as he had a couple of days off to look after Mrs King, who was ill. 'Great,' he said. 'I wish I could come too. Of course you can go.'

'We thought it might be too expensive,' said Lucy.

Mr King read the letter again and frowned hard. 'Yes, you're absolutely right. It's much too expensive. Sorry.'

The brightness in their eyes died away and Lucy felt a huge hole opening beneath her feet.

Mrs King called across from her armchair, 'Don't tease them like that, Harold. You are rotten. You can see they believe you.'

Mr King went red and coughed. 'I'm sorry. Of course you can go. I was only pulling your leg – well, two legs really, one each.'

'Fantastic!' yelled Lucy, disappearing upstairs.

'Now where has she gone?' asked her father.

'Can't you hear? She's putting on her roller skates,' said Mrs King, as a series of crashes and thunderous bangs came from the ceiling above. This was followed by a hesitant thud, thud, thud, as Lucy tried to come down the stairs without slipping over.

'Why doesn't she bring them down and then put them on?' asked Dad.

'I'm going to get mine,' cried Nicholas, and he rushed out before he realized that he didn't have any of his own and had always borrowed Lucy's. Even though he was two years younger he was only one shoe size behind her and almost as tall.

He ran outside to watch his sister and see if he could beg a turn off her.

For the rest of the evening the two of them went up and down the pavement until their legs ached. Lucy and Nicholas were not the only ones practising either. That end of town seemed full of children whizzing round on skates, pretending they were on the ice rink.

Paula and Lucy sat next to each other on the coach, until Paula pointed out daringly that Robert was sitting by himself. 'Why don't you sit next to him?' she giggled.

Lucy quickly made up her mind and slid over to Robert. He glanced sideways at her and grinned. Meanwhile Paula began sending frantic signals up and down the coach until everyone knew that Robert and Lucy were sitting beside each other.

Everyone knew except Mr Barber. Somebody gave a low wolf-whistle. Mr Barber turned round. He could sense something in the air but couldn't pin it down. He saw Lucy and Robert sharing their seat, but there was nothing wrong with that and he turned back to the front, while half the coach sniggered and pointed. Lucy got redder and redder. Robert nudged her with his elbow.

'Don't worry. They're just jealous,' he whispered. Lucy sighed and relaxed. Of course they were.

The skating rink was in a strange building made of huge curved sheets of corrugated steel and plastic. The rink was already half-full with other skaters, slipping, sliding, falling over or whizzing expertly round. The children took their shoes off and queued up to swap them for skates – all except Maureen who had already popped on her own swanky pair and was now twirling round the ice. That was the trouble with Maureen, she was always good at everything, especially showing up other people.

Lucy got a bright green pair of skates. She slipped them on easily enough, but the laces were about half a mile long, and there seemed to be a hundred holes in her boots. Mr Barber came over and helped. He tied her boots so tightly she felt as if her legs had been set in plaster.

Lucy waddled on to the ice and fell over instantly. She got up with a laugh and clung to the sides. Nicholas came and joined her.

'It's easy,' he claimed. 'Push with one foot, like on roller skates.' He set off, a bit slow and wobbly, but he didn't fall over. Lucy followed behind. Gradually she began to get the right idea and she speeded up, pushing and sliding and wobbling crazily.

'How do you stop?' she yelled after Nicholas.

'I don't know. Just keep going.' He went off round the curve, while Lucy carried straight on and hit the barrier with a thump that knocked the breath from her. When she managed to turn round she saw Robert go gliding past, skating like a dream. He's really good, thought Lucy. Then he fell over and slid ten metres on his belly.

Lucy pushed from the side and began another weird journey round the rink. Maureen overtook her, hands clasped behind her back and skating smoothly, without effort. Lucy wrinkled her nose and tried to go faster. There was a sudden whoosh as a big teenager went hissing past, slid across to his pals and stopped on the spot, his blades throwing up a shower of ice. Lucy just managed to get her balance back when another youth sliced across her path and knocked her so hard she thumped down on the ice. Lucy sat there with eyes blazing.

Mr Barber came over and helped her up. 'Are you all right?'

'It's those big boys. They go too fast,' she complained. Mr Barber nodded and said she was not the first to be knocked over by them. He skated over to the laughing group and spoke to them. They grinned and shook their heads. One by one they skated away, not even bothering to listen to Mr Barber. He was left by himself. He shrugged at their rudeness and carried on round the rink, keeping an eye on things.

Paula came past and Lucy grabbed her hand. It was easier and more fun when you had somebody to hold on to, and Paula was quite good. They went round three times without falling over, until two lads came racing up behind and dived beneath the girls' arms. They fell in a tangled heap on the hard ice.

'Those boys are spoiling it for everybody,' said Paula, as she struggled to her feet. 'Let's go to the cafeteria. It's safer there.'

Most of the school was in the cafe. They had all got fed up with the big lads. Lucy wished that there was something she could do, but as yet she had no ideas at all.

They went back on the ice for one last session before home-time. Lucy's skating improved quite a lot. She fell over twice and was knocked over five times. Even Maureen was sent sprawling by one of the lads as he charged along in the wrong direction. Then Mr Barber called the children off the ice and said it was time to get the coach back to school. Lucy collected her shoes and wandered over to the barrier to watch the skaters that were left. The big lads now had the rink to themselves. They were zooming about, twisting, turning and generally showing off. Lucy watched angrily. She could feel her eyes blazing and knew just what power was surging inside her.

Lucy quickly glanced around to see if anyone was watching her. Paula came over. 'Are you coming?' she asked.

'Shhh!' hissed Lucy. 'I'm concentrating!' Her eyes narrowed to tiny red dots and her body crackled. Sparks began to leap from her hair and sizzle on the ice. Paula stepped back, half frightened, half amazed. There was a strange melting smell. Lucy glowed more and more until all at once the whole ice rink melted under her fierce gaze.

Startled yells and loud splashes brought people running to the rink. There was hardly any ice left, just one or two small icebergs, cheerfully bobbing on the surface, while the boys were now slopping about in a pool of chilled water. They were soaked through and kept catching their skates in the copper cooling tubes as they tried to wade to the side.

'What's happened?' croaked the attendant. 'I don't understand it!' He hurried off to check the refrigeration plant.

Paula knew it was nothing to do with that and all down to Lightning Lucy. She watched her friend smooth back her curls and saw the last sparks fade away. Mr Barber was leaning over the barrier, staring at the giant puddle. Trying not to smile, he watched the youths crash through the water and struggle out. Then he looked at Lucy King. She winked at him.

Mr Barber put his hands on his hips and tried to be cross, but it was no use. 'Lucy King . . .' he began, but could think of nothing more to say except, 'Get on that coach and let's go home before they ask too many questions.'

Lucy grinned and went and sat next to Robert for the journey home.

4 The Sound of Music

Mrs Ruddlestone was Lucy's piano teacher. She
was a tall, thin lady who wore tall, thin dresses
that came down to her ankles. She had very
large eyes and while Lucy played, Mrs
Ruddlestone would sit next to her, staring at the
ceiling. Sometimes Lucy would stop and look at
the ceiling too. It was a mystery to her what Mrs
Ruddlestone found up there.

Mrs Ruddlestone gave a long, long sigh. 'Lucy,
dear, you do understand that the Music Festival
is tomorrow afternoon?'

'Yes.'

'There will be other children there and I am
sure they will be playing *Ten Tin Soldiers* quite
beautifully. I'm afraid you will sound rather

strange if you play like you are now. You must practise – hard.' Mrs Ruddlestone pressed a thin hand to her forehead. 'Now I have a headache. I shall meet you at the Town Hall at two o'clock tomorrow.' The piano teacher stood up and her long thin dress rustled and unfolded, length after length. She stalked gently from the room. Lucy could hear her talking to Mrs King. Lucy sat on the stool and waited.

Mrs King came in, her arms folded. 'Don't you want to learn the piano?' she asked. 'Mrs Ruddlestone is most upset. She was so sure you could manage that piece for the Festival.'

'It's boring,' muttered Lucy. 'I want to make my fingers whizz up and down and make brilliant sounds, like they do at concerts and things.'

'I know you do, Lucy, but you are trying to run before you can walk.'

'I can walk!' cried Lucy.

'You know what I mean. You cannot play the piano like that until you've learnt *how* to play. You start with simple things, even if they are boring. If you keep practising you will get better and then you can move on to harder, more interesting pieces.' Mrs King sighed. 'All those other children will be there tomorrow. It wouldn't be fair to spoil it for them by playing badly.'

Lucy scowled. 'They're probably so bored they've fallen asleep in their lessons. They've probably got so fed up they've gone into a coma and can't be woken up ever!'

Mrs King began to laugh. 'Never mind, give it one more go. I'm going upstairs to sort out some clothes for hospital.'

Lucy turned back to the music but she couldn't concentrate. She kept thinking about her mother going into hospital. It was because of the pains she had been having recently. The hospital tests had shown that she would need a minor operation. Mum and Dad said it was quite straightforward, and Mum would only be in hospital for three or four days. Then she would come home and have to rest for a while. Even so, Lucy could not help thinking about it and worrying.

Mr King came home at lunch time because it was a special occasion. 'Fancy my daughter playing in a festival!' he said as they had lunch, and he smiled encouragingly across the table. Lucy did not feel at all encouraged and she was certain, deep in her fluttering heart, that the whole afternoon was going to be a first-class disaster.

As soon as lunch was over she was sent upstairs to wash and change. She splashed a bit of water over her hands and face and then found a dress. That had already caused one argument. Lucy wanted to wear dungarees, but her mother had insisted she put on her best frilly white dress, *and* wear a bow in her hair.

'Cor!' cried Nicholas. 'You look smart! Like a princess!'

Lucy looked daggers at him and stamped downstairs.

'That looks lovely,' said Mrs King.

'It does make a difference,' agreed her father. 'I don't think I've seen you in a dress for at least a year.'

'It's horrible,' Lucy snarled.

'Let's see your hands,' said Mrs King, turning Lucy's palms up. 'What did you wash them with – mud? Go and wash them properly and scrub your nails this time!' Lucy stamped back upstairs again. This was obviously going to be the worst day in her entire life, and she was only nine years old.

They piled into the car and drove to the Town

Hall. Already there were crowds wandering round outside. Mothers and fathers called to their children as they tried to sort out where they were supposed to go. Everybody seemed worried and serious. A long, tall figure came striding across to the Kings.

'Ah, there you are, Lucy!' said Mrs Ruddlestone. 'I'm glad you could come. Now, this must be Nicholas.' She beamed down at Lucy's brother. 'What a lovely bow tie you're wearing.'

'It's not a real one,' explained Nicholas. 'It's on elastic. Look.' He pulled the red bow tie so it came away from his collar. There was a loud twang as the elastic snapped and Nicholas was left holding the broken tie in one hand. 'Oh,' he said softly.

Mrs King sighed. 'Never mind, I've got a safety pin to fix it. Come on, Nicholas. Let's go and find our seats.'

Mrs Ruddlestone beamed again. 'Yes, yes. You go and get your places. I'll look after Lucy.' She began to guide Lucy through the crowd until they reached a small gathering by a door. 'Now we are all here,' said Mrs Ruddlestone. 'Has everyone got their music?' The children piled through the door chattering excitedly.

'I'm doing a solo,' said a tall, fair-haired boy called Jason.

'Are you? I couldn't! You are brave,' whispered one of the girls.

'I should get a prize,' Jason added airily. 'Mrs Ruddlestone says I'm brilliant. I expect I shall go to Music School and become a famous concert pianist.' He turned to Lucy, standing there in her dazzling frilly white dress and velvet hair ribbon. 'What are you going to do?' Jason asked. 'Will you become a concert pianist?'

'I'm going to be a footballer,' said Lucy huskily and everyone began to laugh. She coloured.

'I am!' she insisted.

Jason sniggered. 'She's mad. Come on. Let's go and see the stage. I want to see what make the grand piano is. I hope it's a good one. I've got a Steinway grand at home, but it's not full size. I'm saving up for a proper one.' Away went Jason, his fair head bobbing above the crowd.

Lucy glared after them. She wished she could get away. She felt like zooming into the air, crashing up through the domed ceiling of the Town Hall and flying away for ever, until she reached a desert island where pianos had never been heard of, and the only music was the sound of the sea rippling on to the hot, sunny beach and a warm breeze ruffling the palm trees.

'Lucy!' called Mrs Ruddlestone. 'Come and sit here with the others.'

They sat near the stage. Lucy looked out into the audience but she couldn't spot her family anywhere. Her group was called to play their piece almost at once. There were ten pianos lined up on stage. Mrs Ruddlestone turned to the audience. 'Now we are going to hear a piece called *Ten Tin Soldiers*,' she announced. 'One, two, three . . .'

The march began. Ten pianos were playing beautifully together. Lucy held her breath. She was doing it! She glanced down at her fingers and began to panic. There was so many of them. How could she control all those wiggly fingers at the same time? Now nine pianos were playing together and one soldier had gone off course. His legs were crumpling and folding. Lucy looked at her music in despair. It was hopeless. She put her fingers down anywhere, everywhere, hoping to hit the right note.

'Stop! Stop!' hissed Mrs Ruddlestone. The other players had finished long ago and Lucy had been struggling on by herself without even realizing. The children got up, bowed stiffly and left the stage while the audience clapped politely.

'You ruined it!' snarled Jason, sitting next to Lucy. 'You ruined it for everybody. We were all perfect. It was only you!'

Lucy hardly listened. She wasn't worried about the others. She was concerned about her mum and dad who had come all this way to listen to her and she'd mucked up the whole thing. It was unbearable. Lucy sat, sunk in gloom, while the Festival went on, and on.

Thirty recorder players got up and creaked and squeaked their way through endless dreary pieces. Children with violins that could hardly be squeezed beneath their chins stood in long rows and scraped away. The audience clapped half-heartedly and looked at their watches.

Lucy sat, chin in both hands, staring glumly at the floor. 'It's no wonder you want to be a footballer,' muttered Jason. 'It sounded as if you were playing that piano with football boots on.'

Mrs Ruddlestone made another announcement. 'A special treat,' she began. 'My star pupil, Jason Mullet, will play for you.'

Jason mounted the steps to much clapping. He

bowed, with a rather smug grin on his face. Lucy sat and watched. Jason sat at the grand piano and rolled back his sleeves. He adjusted the height of the piano stool and smoothed the music. Lucy was beginning to get rather a wicked idea.

Jason stared at the ceiling just like Mrs Ruddlestone and raised both hands to start. Just as he brought down his hands the piano lid slammed shut, and he banged out the first chord on the wood. There was a gasp from the audience. Jason opened the lid carefully and checked it. He raised both hands to start again. This time, the whole piano slid away from him. His hands whooshed through the air silently and hit his knees. Lucy giggled quietly, and hoped nobody would notice her crackling away on her seat.

Mrs Ruddlestone stared hard at the piano and shook her head. It was a mystery to her. Jason pulled his stool over to the piano and warily began to play. Lucy watched and waited. This would teach him not to make fun of her! Slowly, the piano began to slide away from the stool. Jason leaned forward, stretching out his arms to reach the retreating piano. He fell off the stool.

The audience began to buzz, wondering what was going on. Mrs Ruddlestone made some kind of excuse, while Jason glared at the piano and marched off stage. But even while this was taking place there was a gasp from the audience as Lucy went zooming into the air, trailing glittering sparks like little fireworks in her wake.

'It's Lightning Lucy! Didn't recognize her in that dress. What's she going to do?'

A moment later the excited audience found out. Down on the stage the grand piano rumbled and creaked and slowly lifted into the air, shimmering in a red glow as Lucy raised it until it hovered beneath the big domed roof. She swooped up to the piano and began to play *Ten Tin Soldiers*, hovering in mid-air.

It was not a perfect performance. In fact there were a lot of mistakes, but the audience didn't notice. They were too busy enjoying the wonderful spectacle of the flying pianist. It certainly made the Music Festival much more exciting.

Lucy finished the piece and came back to earth with a little bump. Mr and Mrs King were waiting, not at all pleased.

'You did that to Jason, didn't you?' said her father angrily. 'It was very unkind.'

But Lucy didn't think so. Jason was so big-headed he would soon get over it, and he had been rather nasty to her. Besides, the concert was so boring until she had done her party-piece.

Nicholas came up and whispered to her. 'That was fantastic,' he said, 'but you still made too many mistakes.'

5 Time for a Shower

Mr and Mrs King soon forgot about the Music Festival. They had their minds taken up with more important matters as Mrs King prepared to go into hospital for her operation. She kept writing out long lists of what would need doing in the house while she was away. 'Don't let the washing pile up,' she said.

'I won't,' said her husband.

'And make sure the ironing gets done.'

'Stop worrying. I'll see to it. Have you got everything you need? Toothbrush? Suitcase?'

Mrs King nodded. The whole family felt on edge. After all, it was not every day that one of them went into hospital for an operation. As they got in the car Mrs King turned to Lucy with a ghost of a smile. 'Now I know how you felt when you had to play that piece of music on stage,' she said. 'I've got butterflies in my stomach.'

Mr King laughed. 'It's no wonder you're having an operation. Poor things – fancy fluttering about down in your insides.'

The hospital seemed modern from the outside, but inside it was just like any other, with a tangy smell of antiseptic and disinfectant everywhere. A nursing sister showed them to the right ward.

'This will be your bed, Mrs King. If your family would like to wait outside for a few minutes, you can get your bedclothes on and make yourself comfortable.' The nurse pulled thick curtains round Mrs King's bed and she vanished from view.

Lucy, Nicholas and Mr King waited outside, sitting uncomfortably on the edge of their seats. They sat in silence, unable to think of anything to say to each other. All their thoughts were with Mrs King. It seemed ages before the sister came to the door and invited them back into the ward. The screen had been pushed back, and Mrs King was sitting up in bed, smiling. 'I feel silly, sitting in bed in the middle of the day,' she said.

'You don't look silly,' answered her husband.

'Don't forget to buy some eggs, will you?' reminded Mrs King, still worrying about how they would manage. 'And don't forget onions either.'

Mr King bent forward and kissed his wife's cheek. 'We're not idiots,' he said. 'Stop fretting. We'll be fine.'

All too soon it was time to leave. The doctor came to examine Mrs King, and the rest of the family were told to go home and come back in the evening, when the operation was over. They kissed their mother goodbye and walked out of the ward, feeling very strange as they left her behind.

'I hope she'll be all right,' murmured Lucy.

'Of course she will. You'll see, when we come back this evening. Now, let's get home. Mum's going to be away a few days and when she gets back I want her to have a surprise.'

'What sort of surprise?'

Mr King grinned at the children. 'We are going to put a shower unit in the bathroom,' he announced. 'We're going to add extra piping to carry the hot and cold water. We shall have to tile some of the walls in the corner and put in a shower-tray. I've already bought that and hidden it in the garage. Then we connect up the shower, put in a curtain rail, a curtain and hey presto!'

'Is it really as easy as that?' asked Lucy.

'Of course it is,' said their father confidently. He had never put up tiles, or showers, nor done any plumbing before. 'It will be such a nice coming-home present for Mum.'

Mr King was also thinking that the work would help keep everyone's minds off the operation.

When they reached home Mr King showed them the shower-tray. It was made of moulded blue plastic. He pushed it into one corner of the bathroom and explained where everything had to go. First of all they had to put in the plumbing. That meant two new sections of copper tubing had to be connected to the pipes under the bath.

Mr King went downstairs and turned the mains water supply off, so they could cut holes in the pipes without drowning themselves.

He shone a torch under the bath. 'Hmmm. There are lots of pipes here,' he called out. 'But

I'm sure I know which one is which. Pass me one of those special adaptor valves, Nicholas.'

Mr King began to bang and thump. He shouted 'Ow!' several times and one or two other words that shouldn't be written down. Lucy and Nicholas sat on the edge of the bath grinning at each other. Every so often they passed down some copper tubing, or more valves, and gradually two long snakes of copper pipe came out from beneath the bath and wriggled their way to the shower tray and up the wall. Mr King fixed the shower unit on the end.

'We'd better test it before I fix it to the wall properly,' he said. 'Turn the mains on downstairs.'

Lucy ran down and turned the tap back on. Water gurgled round and round the pipes, filling the tanks in the loft.

Mr King turned on the shower. Nothing happened.

'I don't understand,' he grumbled. He tried the bath taps, but only the hot tap worked and that delivered cold water. Mr King scratched his head. He pulled the lavatory chain to see if that still flushed properly. It did, but with hot water. Steam billowed from the bowl.

Lucy and Nicholas were giggling madly, while Mr King wandered round the bathroom wondering what had gone wrong.

'I'm going to call a plumber,' he snapped at last. 'Come on, it's time we went back to the hospital.' He stalked off downstairs.

'Not a word about this to your mother,' he said in the car. 'It's going to be a surprise.'

Lucy said it probably would be a surprise when Mum found hot water flushing the loo bowl.

Mrs King was sitting up in bed, waiting for them. She was propped up on four big pillows, and although she looked pale, she was wide awake and smiling.

'Are you all right?' asked Lucy.

'Can I see the cut?' demanded Nicholas immediately.

Mum started to laugh and quickly winced. 'Ouch. It hurts when I laugh. It pulls on the stitches. I'll show you when I come home and the dressing has been taken off. I haven't even seen it myself yet.'

Mr King sat on the edge of the bed and asked how the whole operation had gone. Apparently the doctor had already been round and told Mrs

King that it was quite simple and successful. 'So,' went on Mrs King, 'no more awful tummy-pains or backache. And I can come home in two days if I start to heal well.'

Mr King's jaw dropped. 'Two days! That doesn't give us much time.'

'Time for what?' Mrs King was very puzzled.

'Oh, you know,' said her husband, hurriedly trying to think of something.

'He's worried about the ironing,' said Lucy, coming to her father's rescue.

'I told you not to let it pile up,' reminded Mrs King.

They left her some fruit and flowers and went home feeling much happier, now they could see that their mother was getting better and the worst was over.

'Two days doesn't give us much time to finish that shower,' said Mr King. 'We'd better get a move on.'

As soon as they opened the front door Mr King knew something was wrong. There was water pouring down the stairs for a start. He gave a yell and dashed up to the bathroom. There were more yells, a sudden crash of splintering wood and a scream. Something shattered on the kitchen floor and Lucy ran in to find water cascading down through a large hole in the ceiling. There was her father, jammed in the hole, his legs wriggling about and water pouring down around him. A muffled shout came from above. 'Help! Turn the water off, ooof! Get me out!'

Nicholas joined in. 'Lucy, come up here, quick!'

Lucy half ran, half flew upstairs and dashed into the bathroom. Water was spraying out all over the place from the new shower unit. Lucy was instantly soaked to the skin, like the others.

'Keep back!' yelled their father. 'The floor must have been rotten and the water's made it go soggy. That's why I fell through. I'm stuck. Stop the water!'

Lucy stared at the pipe where the water was spraying out. Her eyes went red and tiny. She focused her fierce glare on the copper pipe, slowly welding over the hole until the spray stopped.

'Well done,' panted her father. 'Get a plank from the garage and lay it across the floor.'

Nicholas raced downstairs and came struggling back with a plank, which they pushed in front of their father. He rested his arms on it and gradually pulled himself clear of the hole and crawled to the bathroom door. They sat on the floor looking at the soggy mess.

'I don't think this is the kind of shower Mum would like,' said Mr King.

'I wish I'd had a camera,' said Lucy. 'You looked really funny with your legs hanging through the kitchen ceiling.'

Her father groaned. 'There isn't mess down there too, is there?'

Lucy nodded. Mr King gave another groan and went down to investigate. He squelched out of the kitchen looking very depressed. 'I shall have to phone the builder as well as the plumber. I give up. I should have got them in straight away. This will probably turn out to be the most expensive shower in the history of bathrooms.'

'Can't we do the tiling?' asked Nicholas hopefully.

'I don't think so. The way our luck is going the whole wall will fall down if we so much as lay a finger on it. I hope the builder can finish before Mum comes home.'

It was a strange house they slept in that night. It was probably the only place in the country with a hot-water lavatory, cold bath and a hole through to the room below.

'If Mum sees this I should think she'll turn round and go straight back to the hospital,' said Lucy, as she went to bed.

'I think I'll join her,' groaned her father. 'Goodnight, Lucy, and thanks for your help. I didn't know you could weld metal like that.'

Lucy grinned up at her father. 'Neither did I,' she admitted. 'But there's a first time for everything, isn't there?'

'First *and* last for my plumbing,' grunted Dad.

6 The Home Help

When Mrs King came home from hospital the house was clean and tidy. The shower was in place, the hole in the floor was mended, the ironing and washing had all been done. A builder friend of Mr King had seen to the bathroom. It had cost quite a lot of money but Mr King was secretly pleased that he hadn't had to sort out the problems himself. The shower cubicle looked splendid, and it really was a surprise for Mrs King.

'My goodness! Did you do that?' was her first question.

'Well yes . . .' began her husband.

'And no . . .' added Nicholas, honestly.

'We did some of it,' said Lucy. 'Mostly the first bit.'

Mrs King looked from one to another, not knowing what to make of it.

'What was the first bit?' she asked.

'The most difficult bit,' said Nicholas.

'The most exciting bit,' added Lucy, grinning. Again Mrs King looked from one to another, feeling slightly confused. She did think that the shower looked very nice and said she couldn't wait to use it.

'One day we shall tell you the whole story,' said her husband, 'but not quite yet, because we haven't recovered from it yet, have we?'

Nicholas and Lucy agreed, although Lucy was rather sad that the lavatory had been put right. She secretly wished that it still flushed hot water. The doctor came to the house and told them that Mrs King would have to rest for some time and take only a little exercise at first. No housework for a while.

'Oh, good,' smiled Mrs King. The doctor didn't laugh.

'I mean it, Mrs King. You must find someone to come in and clean and cook for you. Perhaps your husband and children can help?'

'Of course we will,' said Lucy. 'We're good at helping.'

'I have a couple more days off before I have to go back to work,' said Mr King. 'We'll sort out a routine and follow that. It shouldn't be too difficult.'

Mrs King was already closing her eyes, half asleep. The doctor said she would be like that for a while. 'It's the anaesthetic wearing off. She'll be tired for two or three weeks and then get back to normal quite quickly.' She packed her case and left, while Mrs King fell fast asleep on the settee.

The rest of the family sat down and tried to work out a plan. Nicholas said he would make breakfast and tidy bedrooms. Lucy offered to sort out washing, change the beds and vacuum the carpets.

'That's fine,' agreed their father. 'I'll sit back and watch you both.'

'You can't!' yelled Lucy and Nicholas together.

'Ssssh,' said their father. 'You'll wake Mum.'

'I am awake,' she said, opening one eye. 'Dad can cook lunch and tea, do the washing-up and the drying-up, rinse the basins, feed the cats, do the ironing and . . .'

'Hold on, hold on, that's not fair,' wailed Mr King.

'Yes it is. You're twice as big as the children, so you can do twice as much. Now stop disturbing my beauty sleep.'

'I'll send you back to hospital if you go on like that,' warned Mr King.

The children started out well. Nicholas did have one or two problems with breakfast. He burnt the toast and made the tea with sugar in the teapot, but it made life more interesting. At length though they got bored with picking up bits of dirty clothing and endlessly cleaning and tidying.

Lucy was fed up with pushing the vacuum cleaner round and round, and tried to think of a more exciting way of doing the housework.

First of all she concentrated her powers on the vacuum cleaner. She sat back in a nice comfy armchair while she made the cleaner wander backwards and forwards over the carpet. She called Nicholas in to watch, and as soon as he came in she made the vacuum cleaner chase him round the room, with the nozzle waving in mid-air and sucking at his pullover. He was not impressed.

'It's all right for you, but I can't do things like that.'

Lucy carried on controlling the cleaner.

'What I need,' Nicholas complained, 'is a robot to do my work. I'm worn out.'

Lucy thought a robot sounded a great idea and was so busy thinking about it that she forgot to keep her thoughts on the vacuum cleaner. Before she knew what was happening, it had swallowed the tablecloth and climbed halfway up the wall. She brought it back to the ground and switched it off quickly.

It was then Lucy realized she hadn't seen Colonel for some time.

Nicholas stared at his sister in horror. 'You haven't sucked the kitten into the vacuum cleaner, have you?'

Lucy bit her lip. 'I don't think so. I'm sure I would have noticed.'

Nicholas seized the machine and ripped off the lid. He tipped out the dust bag and a cloud of filth billowed into the air.

'Urgh!' coughed Lucy and at that moment she heard a little mew. There was the kitten, clutching on to the topmost bookshelf where he had dashed to escape the roaring vacuum monster. Lucy lifted him down and took him through to a quieter room. Then they set about clearing up the mess they had just made. When that was finished Lucy said she would help her brother with the washing-up.

Lucy had a strange way of tackling it. The dirty plates were by the side of the sink and Lucy made them fly round the room, one by one, before divebombing into the washing-up bowl and sending showers of soap suds over the edge. After a quick dip the plates took off once more, this time with Nicholas in hot pursuit, waving a tea-towel and desperately trying to dry them.

Unfortunately Lucy got a little too clever and tried to make six plates fly in formation, like the Red Arrows. The experiment got a bit out of control and three plates crash-landed in bits, while the other three wobbled dangerously on, and were only saved by Nicholas snatching them from mid-air as they passed over his head.

Mrs King came in to see what the noise was. Lucy was on her knees with the dustpan and brush, clearing up broken plates.

'What happened?' asked Mrs King.

'Three of the plates slipped,' Lucy mumbled.

Her mother wondered how and why the plates had slipped. She was pretty sure she could make a good guess. She was quite used to Lucy's awkward powers. Besides, she could still see a vague glow round Lucy's hands.

'Try and do the washing-up normally, Lucy. Then you're unlikely to break any more plates. You're supposed to be helping.'

Lucy finished off washing-up the boring way, while her mother went to lie down.

A little later, Nicholas came from the hall with some post that had just been delivered. 'There's a letter for me,' he said, surprised.

'I never get any letters,' Lucy moaned.

'You never write to anybody,' Nicholas said.

'Neither do you.'

'But I've still got a letter,' said Nicholas as he opened it, pulling out a large sheet of paper. He began to read.

'What does it say?' asked Lucy, trying to peer over his shoulder.

'I don't know. I can't read half the words. They're too long.' He held it so that Lucy could see and she began to mouth the words quietly to herself, gradually getting louder as she got more excited. '. . . and your answer was picked out first from the postbag. We are therefore delighted to inform you that you have won the prize of a day-

trip to France for a family of four . . . Nicholas!
It's that Spot the Difference Competition! We've
won it!'

'Oh, wow!' breathed Nicholas, taking back the
letter. 'I don't believe it. I've never been to
France. Can you speak French?'

Lucy shook her head. 'Let's see when we can
go.' She read through the letter again. 'It says we
can take the trip at our own convenience. What
does that mean?'

Nicholas didn't know, and he suggested they
asked their mother. They dashed madly upstairs
and burst into her room. She was half asleep but
the children soon had her eyes wide open.

'How lovely,' she said. 'I've always wanted to
go to France. You're very clever, Nicholas.'

'I did it too,' Lucy insisted.

'Dad will be pleased. As soon as I'm recovered
we'll go over to Boulogne for the day. That will
be something to look forward to.'

Mrs King allowed her head to sink back
against the pillow. 'I feel so tired still. Let me get
a bit of sleep now. You did say you would change
all the beds today before Dad got in. See if you
can give him a double surprise and get that
done, as well as telling him the other great news.'

Mrs King smiled at them both, closed her eyes and went back to sleep as they raced off.

Changing the beds was tiring work for the children. Each bed had to be stripped down and have fresh sheets. When they reached their mother's room they realized they had a problem. She was still fast asleep.

'How can we change that one?' asked Nicholas.

'Watch.' Lucy's hair crackled faintly and she pointed her hands at her mother. Bit by bit Mrs King rose into the air, with a blanket trailing round her. She was snoring quietly.

'Quick!' whispered Lucy. 'Get those covers off and change them.'

Nicholas grabbed the covers and whipped them off. He spread a fresh sheet and tucked it in. Lucy kept her mother hovering near the ceiling until the bed was finished, then slowly brought her back down. Nicholas gave his sister a silent thumbs-up sign and they crept from the room, leaving their mother still fast asleep and none the wiser.

Only when they were safely out of earshot did they collapse into hysterical laughter and then rush outside to find something even more exciting than housework to do.

7 Food for Thought

'I can hardly believe this,' said Mr King, as they drove to Dover. 'Here we are, setting off for France with free tickets, all because Nicholas spotted ten things wrong in a competition.'

'I found some of them,' Lucy reminded everyone.

'Only another fifteen miles,' said Mrs King, glancing at a passing signpost. 'I'm getting excited. I do hope the sea's calm. The last time I went in a boat was a bit of a disaster.'

'Why? What happened?' asked Nicholas.

'It was when your dad and I were young. We went to a boating lake and . . .'

'Yes,' interrupted Mr King. 'The children don't want to hear about that.'

'Oh yes we do!' Lucy and Nicholas shouted.

'Your father hired a rowing boat and I thought he was really manly. He made me sit in the middle of the boat while he got the oars and sat up one end, but he couldn't find anywhere to put the oars . . .'

Lucy started giggling.

'Then your dad realized I was supposed to sit at the end and he had to go in the middle. So we changed places and he almost fell overboard . . .'

'No I didn't!'

'Yes you did. Anyhow, he put the oars in those horseshoe things . . .'

'Rowlocks,' snapped Mr King.

'And shoved the oars in the water. He pulled so hard he fell over backwards into the bottom of the boat. All I could see were two legs waving in mid-air.'

Nicholas laughed out loud and Lucy was about to say that it sounded like the time Dad tried to put a shower in the bathroom and fell through the floor. She stopped herself in the nick of time.

'We spent most of the afternoon going round and round in circles. Eventually he dropped one of the oars and it floated away. So he paddled

after it and tried to grab it with the other oar . . .
until he dropped that one too. Then we heard a
voice shouting, "Come in, Number Four, your
time is up!" I told Dad we had to go back and he
said how could we get back without any oars?'

The two children were doubled up. Lucy had
tears rolling down her cheeks, while their father
angrily drove faster and faster.

'It's not that funny,' he fumed.

'It is, it is!' screamed Lucy.

'What happened?' asked Nicholas.

'They sent out another boat and towed us
back,' laughed Mrs King. 'But that wasn't the
end of it. I got out of the boat and when your
dad tried to follow, he tripped over that
horseshoe thing you put the oar . . .'

'The rowlock!' shouted Mr King again.

'. . . and fell straight into the pond!'

By this time they were laughing so much they
hardly heard Mr King announce in a chilly voice
that they had reached the port. He slowed down
and handed over the passports for checking.

'There it is!' shouted Nicholas. 'That big white
one. You can see its funnel behind the crane.'
They went slowly up a long ramp and down the
other side. Before they even realized, they were

inside the belly of the ferry and were being shown where to stop. As they got out they could see car after car driving on to the boat behind them. Mr King locked up and they made their way to one of the big lounges. Mrs King made herself comfortable next to a low table and the family sat down. Nicholas immediately got up again.

'I'm going to explore,' he announced.

'Me too,' said Lucy, jumping to her feet.

'Don't get lost,' warned their father hopefully, as the two children ran off. He turned back to his wife. 'Peace at last.'

Lucy and Nicholas managed to explore the entire boat in about ten minutes. They went upstairs and downstairs from bow to stern, and finally settled for peering over the back to see when the great ropes that moored the ferry would be cast off. The boat gave a blast on her siren and the dockers began uncurling the ropes. They were thrown into the sea and winches pulled them up on board.

'We're moving!' yelled Lucy, as the boat slowly rocked away from the jetty and began to gather pace. She raced back to the lounge and skidded up to her parents. 'We're moving!' she screamed, turned tail and raced back to Nicholas.

'What was that about peace?' asked Mrs King.

Almost two hours later, France was sighted and the ferry pulled into Boulogne harbour. 'It looks just like England,' Nicholas complained.

'That sign isn't in English,' said his father. 'Come on. Let's go down to the car. Remember, this is France we are in. Nobody will understand our English, and, Lucy . . .'

'What?'

'Please remember that nobody here knows about your special powers. Don't use them.'

Lucy nodded. She was only half listening, being too busy watching the front of the ship open up so that the vehicles could drive off.

They were soon on the move once more. They left the boat behind and drove along the jetty. They kept passing red signs in French.

'What do they mean?' asked Nicholas. All at once a huge French truck came thundering straight at them, horn blaring and lights flashing.

'Drive on the other side of the road!' Mrs King yelled and her husband swerved wildly.

'Phew! That's what those signs meant. I forgot the French drive on the right.'

Going rather slowly they managed to reach the centre of the old French town without being hooted at too often. They found a place to park and then took to their feet, feeling much safer that way. They began to enjoy themselves at last. It was really fun. All the shops were the same as English ones, but different. You could go to the baker but it wasn't called that and it sold different types of bread. The butcher looked the same at first, but then they noticed the meat was different somehow.

Eventually they found a little restaurant where they decided to have lunch. Mrs King picked up the menu and stared at it. 'I can't understand it,' she said. 'It's all in French.' At last a waiter came over and spoke quickly. He was obviously waiting for an order. Mr King looked at him in alarm, wondering how he could even begin to explain.

But the waiter smiled and nodded.

'Ah – English?' he asked.

'Yes!' said Mr King, with great relief.

'I will read you the menu,' said the waiter, and bit by bit he went through the different dishes, while the Kings licked their lips, or pulled horrible faces.

'And this is Frog's Legs in Sauce,' he said. 'And this is tiny – how do you say – sheeps?'

'Tiny sheep?' murmured Mrs King. 'Do you mean lambs? Baaa baaa?'

'No no!' laughed the waiter. 'I mean how you say – shreeps? Sheemps?'

'Shrimps!' Lucy shouted suddenly. 'He means shrimps!'

'Yes, yes, shreemps,' went on the waiter.

'I'm sorry we can't speak any French,' Mrs King said.

'Doesn't matter, doesn't matter.' The waiter wrote down their order.

Mr King leaned across the table and whispered at Lucy, 'Do you really want snails in garlic butter? It sounds revolting. Remember that we have to go back on the boat soon. We don't want you being sick all over the place.'

'I like snails,' said Lucy.

'You've never had them!'

'But I do like them.'

When the snails arrived Lucy was not so certain. Seven big shells sat on her plate. They looked as if they were about to get up and slide off at any moment. The others sat and watched her. They had chosen simple things like chicken or 'shreemps'.

Lucy poked one of the snails gingerly with her

fork. It toppled over. She looked at her mother. 'How do you get it out?' she whispered.

'Here, snail! Here, boy!' coaxed Nicholas, bending over a shell.

'Stop it at once,' snapped their mother. 'Try using your fork, Lucy.'

Lucy held the shell with one hand and tried to lever her fork inside. She struggled for ages, twisting her fork every way until suddenly the snail shot out of the shell, whizzed right across the restaurant and hit the window. There it stuck, slowly slipping down further and further, leaving a trail of garlic butter. Lucy pretended that nothing had happened, even though half the restaurant was now staring in her direction.

'Lucy!' hissed her mother.

'I couldn't help it. It wouldn't come out.' She tried again on a second snail, but that was just as difficult. This time the whole snail, shell and all, shot across the table and got Mr King on the chest.

'Thank you,' he said stonily. 'If I had wanted snails I would have ordered them.' He wiped his greasy shirt with a napkin.

Lucy decided she needed a bit of extra help. She glared hard at a snail shell on her plate, feeling the power gathering in her eyes. She was getting good at controlling it by now and knew just how much force to put into her startling fireball gaze. The shell began to sizzle and crack, then it fell away from the meat inside. Lucy heaved a sigh, stuck her fork in and ate the snail in its sauce of garlic butter. The others watched as she chewed, rolling the food round her cheeks. Lucy closed her eyes.

'It's delicious!' she murmured. 'Utterly delicious!' She opened her eyes and pushed a shell over to her father. 'You try. They're gorgeous!'

'Er, no thank you, Lucy. Not this time. I'm full,' said Mr King lamely.

'I'll try,' said her mother.

So Lucy concentrated her gaze again and split open another shell, handing over the meat to Mrs King.

'I must say, they're not at all bad,' agreed Mrs King a moment later.

Lucy managed to get all the shells open the same way. Several people stared at her very hard, but they couldn't quite believe it. They told themselves there wasn't really a girl smashing up snail shells with her eyebeams. By the time the

Kings left, the whole restaurant was talking about the mystery. Whatever would Lightning Lucy do next?

8 A Case of Mistaken Identity

'We really must go to the hypermarket before we get the ferry back,' said Mr King.

Mrs King was sitting on a low wall, looking out over the harbour.

'What do we want to go there for?' she asked. 'Can't we stay here? My feet are getting tired of all this wandering about.'

'Do you want a lift, Mum?' asked Lucy, with a sly grin.

'No thanks, Lucy. I know just what your *lifts* are like. Before I know it I shall be doing a triple loop and breaking the sound barrier.'

Mr King shuffled his feet impatiently. 'Come on. We've got to catch the ferry in an hour. We haven't much time to collect our duty-free allowance.'

'So that's what all the hurry is about,' cried Mrs King. 'You just want to make sure you have plenty of wine to take back. Typical. Come on then, we'd better get going.'

On the way Mr King explained to Lucy and Nicholas what the duty-free allowance was. 'When you take some things into Britain from another country you have to pay tax on them, because they are much cheaper over here than they are in Britain.'

'What sort of things?' asked Nicholas.

'Wine, perfume, watches, things like that. But, when you're abroad, like we are now, you are allowed to take back a little for yourself without paying the tax, and that's called . . .'

'Duty-free allowance,' finished Lucy.

In the hypermarket the Kings found a whole wall stacked from top to bottom with wine bottles. There were massive crates of beer standing on the floor. People were pulling out crate after crate and throwing them into their trolleys. It was a madhouse, and Dad joined in with a wild grin.

Mrs King looked at the growing pile of wine and beer. 'Is that enough?' she asked at last, a trifle stiffly.

'Just a couple more,' said Dad.

'Don't go over the duty-free limit, will you?' warned Mrs King.

Mr King turned a shade red as he put two more bottles in the trolley. 'One or two extra won't hurt,' he said. 'The Customs officers won't worry about that.'

'Dad!' shouted Lucy. 'Suppose you're arrested?'

'They won't arrest me for two bottles. If they find them, I shall just have to pay the duty on them. That's all.'

Mrs King groaned. 'I smell trouble,' she said.

They caught the ferry with a little time to spare and at last they were able to rest after their long day in Boulogne. Lucy and Nicholas rested for at least three minutes before they went dashing off to see where the front of the ship was, and then where the back of the ship was. Then they went to see what was on one side and then on the other. They explored upstairs, downstairs and were back after twenty minutes, by which time Mr and Mrs King were snoozing in their recliner seats.

The ship's siren woke them as they entered harbour. Passengers were already streaming downstairs to the car decks to get back in their vehicles. Mr King hustled Nicholas and Lucy into the back seat and pushed a rug at his daughter. 'Cover that box with the wine in it, Lucy. With a bit of luck the Customs men will never notice.'

Engines started and cars began to roll off the ferry on to the dock. They came to a large sign which said **NOTHING TO DECLARE** and pointed to the left. Mr King followed the arrow.

'I hope you know what you're doing,' muttered Mrs King anxiously.

'Of course I do. I've only got six extra bottles.'

'Six! I thought you said it was a couple!' Mrs King stared at her husband with eyes like a dragon.

'Yes, well, I made a slight mistake in my adding up . . .' he began.

'Oooh! You ought to be shot!'

'Dad – suppose you get caught?' wailed Nicholas.

'I won't. Look, for heaven's sake, it's only a little extra and I can pay the extra duty.'

At that moment they came to the Customs shed. The cars drove into different lanes and

Customs officers took a quick look at each one and waved them on. Mr King drove up with a cheerful smile. A Customs officer stepped forward and halted the car.

'Anything to declare, sir?'

'No – we've just got the usual wine and beer. That's all.'

The officer peered into the depths of the car. He nodded at Lucy and Nicholas. 'These your children, sir?'

Mr King could not help himself. 'No. I bought them at the hypermarket.'

The officer stared at Mr King icily. 'Very funny, sir. Would you pull your car over there so we can inspect your luggage, please?' And he pointed to where a line of cars were having everything taken out for inspection.

Mr King drove over to the line.

'You stupid idiot!' hissed Mrs King. 'You and your big mouth. You had to be clever-clever, didn't you? Now you'll have to own up about the extra wine and it serves you right.'

The Kings had to get out of the car and a Customs officer stood over them and told them what to unpack. Out came the bags and everything in the bags, out came seats, out came anything that could be taken out, including the case with the rug over the top.

Lucy stared at the case and watched the officer. She had the beginnings of an idea that could just help Dad out of his trouble. Mrs King was busy in the front of the car. Mr King was opening the bonnet. The Customs officer was leaning over the engine.

Lucy's hair began to crackle faintly, little sparks jerked and juddered from her fingertips and the wine case lifted from the ground. Her simple idea was to get it up in the air, out of sight until the inspection was over. Gradually the wine case rose higher and higher, above everyone's head. Lucy smiled. This was easy-peasy!

'Hey! Hey! That's our wine up there!' Suddenly Lucy was thrown to one side as several people came thundering past. They climbed up the Kings' car and tried to get at the flying wine case. Instinctively Lucy made it fly away from them, and a desperate chase began. Others began to shout and join in. People clambered on to car roofs and stampeded across bonnets. They leaped on to other cars and tried to stand on people's shoulders.

Lucy tried to control the crazy case of wine that everybody thought belonged to them, but she was rapidly disappearing in a heaving, shouting mob of travellers. Several people started to climb the iron pillars to the roof. They swung from girders like a troup of baboons as they tried to get their hands on the flying case.

'Oi! That's our case of wine up there!'

'No it isn't! Get your hands off!'

'Hey, stop shoving, you fat twit!'

'Who are you calling a fat twit? Take that!'

The Customs shed was now a mass of wriggling, wrestling, screaming, yelling people. The wine case flew about in uncontrollable loops and dives as Lucy was shoved one way, then another. Whistles blew, sirens wailed and at last there was an almighty crash as the wine case dive-bombed a truck carrying more wine from France. Bottles shattered all over the place and wine poured like Niagara Falls across the concrete floor of the shed.

At once the shouts died away. Everybody stood still. They stared at the growing lake of wine and they sniffed. What a pong! Like a million florist shops! Several Customs officers ran to the truck.

'This isn't wine,' one cried. 'It's perfume. It's a truck-load of perfume in wine bottles. Somebody's trying to smuggle perfume through in wine bottles!'

Lightning Lucy scrambled to her feet and gave her electric hair a little shake. She was just in time to see the truck owners being arrested, and everybody else go back to their cars.

'Did you see that? asked Nicholas excitedly. 'They caught some real smugglers!'

'It was the flying wine case that interested me,' said Mrs King, staring very hard at her daughter.

They were interrupted by a Customs man. 'OK, you can pack your car now and go.'

'Go?' said Mr King in disbelief.

'Oh yes. We've done our work for today. We've been after that perfume-smuggling gang for months. We knew they were getting it into this country to sell cheaply, but we didn't know how. Well, we've got them now.'

Lucy sighed with relief. The Customs officers were so pleased with themselves they had forgotten to ask how the trouble had begun.

Mr King packed up the car and drove away. 'Boy,' he began. 'That was a lucky escape. I thought we were done for.' He gave a smile and started to laugh. 'Six extra bottles of wine!'

'You should be ashamed of yourself,' said Mrs King.

Lucy tapped her father on the shoulder. 'Er, Dad, I'm afraid there's one problem. You see, that case of wine that was flying about, well . . .'

The car screeched to a halt. Dad was as white as a soggy meringue. 'No! It wasn't! But that was ALL my wine! ALL of it! TWELVE bottles!'

'I was trying to help. It seemed like such a simple idea – so easy.'

'So simple it nearly caused a riot,' said Mrs King.

'Twelve bottles,' groaned Dad.

'Poetic justice. It serves you right for trying to cheat,' said Mrs King.

Nicholas was gazing at his big sister. 'You've caught a gang of smugglers,' he said. 'Wow!'

At this, Lucy perked up a bit. She even got a bit big-headed. 'So I have! I caught the perfume-smuggling gang . . . wow!'

Mr King held his head in his hands and moaned.

'Twelve bottles of wine, all gone. Oh wow.'